WATCHERS AT THE SHRINE

Also by Jean Ure

for older readers

Plague 99
(Winner of the Lancashire Book Award)
After the Plague
(previously titled Come Lucky April)

for younger readers

The Ghost that Lived on the Hill
Brenda the Bold *(Banana Books)*

JEAN URE

WATCHERS AT THE SHRINE

MAMMOTH

First published in Great Britain 1994
by Methuen Children's Books Ltd
Published 1995 by Mammoth
an imprint of Reed International Books Ltd
Michelin House, 81 Fulham Road, London SW3 6RB
and Auckland, Melbourne, Singapore and Toronto

Reprinted 1996

Copyright © 1994 Jean Ure

The right of Jean Ure to be identified as author of this
work has been asserted by her in accordance with
the Copyright, Designs and Patents Act 1988

ISBN 0 7497 2394 7

A CIP catalogue record for this title
is available from the British Library

Printed and bound in Great Britain by
BPC Paperbacks Ltd
A member of
The British Printing Company Ltd

This paperback is sold subject to the condition
that it shall not, by way of trade or otherwise,
be lent, resold, hired out, or otherwise circulated
without the publisher's prior consent in any form
of binding or cover other than that in which
it is published and without a similar condition
including this condition being imposed
on the subsequent purchaser.

To the 'In Brief'
reviewing team
of 1993

Chapter One

Hal was down in Long Pasture, playing kickball with the other boys, when he heard his name being called. He turned, reluctant to break off in the middle of a game.

'Hal!'

It was David. What did he want? It was not an official visiting day.

'Hal! Here!' He was beckoning. There was something of urgency in the gesture.

'I'll be right back!' Hal flung it over his shoulder as he sprinted up the slope towards the gate, where David stood waiting. Breathless, he said, 'What is it?'

He didn't mean to be rude, but he could think of only one reason for an unscheduled visit: something must have happened to April. Last time he had come, David had mentioned that she was unwell and that they were worried about her.

'It's not April,' he said, 'is it?'

'No. Hal, listen – ' David gripped his arm. He sounded apologetic, but determined. His face, which was more lined than Hal remembered it from even just a few months ago, was sombre, almost grim.

'I've just come from Central Hall. The vote has gone against us again.'

Hal's immediate reaction was one of impatience: so what? Why pull him out of the game just to tell him that? The vote was always going against them. It was the fourth defeat they had suffered even in Hal's short life, and he knew, from what his sister Keren had told him, that David and April between them had been fighting the community for far longer than that.

His second reaction, selfishly, was one of relief. His life would scarcely be worth living if the vote were ever to go their way. The Boys' House would presumably be closed, or at any rate converted to other uses; they would all be returned to the community before their time, and he would be resented, even though it could hardly be called his fault.

'So how is April?' he said, eager to get back to his game. 'Is she all right?'

'Bitterly disappointed.'

He hadn't meant that: he had meant how was her health. Although she was his mother, Hal had not seen April since entering the Boys' House at the age of twelve. In theory, these days, older women were allowed in, but it would have embarrassed Hal to have his mother visit him. She was already known as an eccentric. She had wept when Hal had gone off with the other boys; Hal had never lived it down.

'I came at once,' said David, 'the minute the result was known. We'd already made plans, just in case. Hal, the fact is that we've decided to pull you out.'

'Pull me out?' Hal was stunned. 'You mean – '

'Just for a short while. We think we can almost certainly manage to swing it next time.'

Hal cried angrily, 'You can't do that to me!'

'I give you my word . . . it won't be for long. They're coming round. We very nearly got there. Just another handful of votes – '

'I've heard all this before!' It was what they had said last time, and the time before that. *Just a handful of votes*. 'You'll never win, you're fighting a lost cause, everybody says so!'

'We shall win,' said David.

'Not before you've gone and ruined everything for me!'

David winced. 'Far from ruining you, we're doing our very best to save you.'

'Save me from what? I don't want to be saved!'

'Hal, we've already been into all this. You know perfectly well what will happen to you if you stay on here.'

'Yes! The same as'll happen to all the others – the same as happened to you! Why do I have to be different? You had your time! Why are you trying to take mine away from me?'

'We're trying to prevent your life from being wrecked!'

'Was yours wrecked?' Hal faced him, challengingly.

'It – could have been other than how it was.'

'I said, *was it wrecked?*' He almost screamed it at him.

'All right! If you want to know the truth, yes! It was wrecked – as yours is not going to be. I'm sorry if we seem to be making some kind of scapegoat of you, but I do promise you, the day will come when you will be grateful.'

'Never! I shall hate you for it, always!' Just

because David and April were a pair of freaks, did that mean they had to make him one, too?

'Hal, please.' David took him by the shoulders and lightly shook him. 'You have to believe me . . . we are doing this for your own good. Any of the others are free to come out if they want to. The choice will be offered them.'

'They won't want to come!' Hal said it scornfully.

'They might if you went and talked to them.'

'I'm not going to talk to them!'

'Then maybe I should.'

Danilo was coming up the slope towards them. He was one of the younger men who had opted to stay in the Boys' House and teach rather than return to the community.

'David!' He held out a hand. 'I just heard the news . . . I'm so sorry.'

Hal stared. *Danilo* was sorry? Did that mean he supported the motion?

'We're taking Hal out,' said David. 'Do I have your permission to go down and have a word with the others?'

'Of course.'

'Wait there, then, Hal, if you'd rather not come with me. I shan't be long.'

Hal watched, frowning, as David made his way down the slope. He saw him stop the kickball game by simply walking into the middle of it. (*That* would make him popular.) He saw the boys gather round, saw their heads start shaking; saw David leave them and walk on into the house.

'I doubt he'll get anywhere,' said Danilo. He sighed. 'It's all-important at your age, isn't it? To be one of the gang? I was just the same. By the time I came to my senses, it was too late. The deed had already been done. You're going to be one of the lucky ones.'

Hal scowled.

'Yes, yes, I know! I'm sure at this moment you don't believe a word I'm saying, but there'll come a day when you'll thank David and April. We could do with a few more like them. It's not everyone who's prepared to go against the entire community for the sake of sticking to their principles. It hasn't made life easy for them.'

No, thought Hal; and it hadn't made his life easy, either.

'Look, I can guess what you're thinking.' Danilo laid a consolatory arm about his shoulders. 'Just now you're suffering because you're the odd one out. But when the time is right you'll come back and take up your place amongst us. Hopefully, in the not-too-distant future.'

'When you say, come back . . . you mean, back here?' Hal waved a hand down into the valley, where the Boys' House nestled in the shelter of the trees.

'Not here! No. I mean back to the community.'

'But – ' The truth slowly dawned on him. He was not only being taken out of the Boys' House: they were actually going to send him away.

'You couldn't stay on in the community, you know.' Danilo said it gently. 'Not without serving your time.'

Not without going through the Boys' House. Not as an uncivilised male. It was what it was all about, this wretched vote that they were so obsessed with. Boys, claimed David and April, should be allowed to grow up side by side with the girls. The act of civilising them was a crime against humanity.

Yes, was the standard retort, and you had only to look back to the final years of the twentieth century to see what came about when they were left uncivilised.

No one disputed that the disastrous plague of 1999, which had come near to wiping out all of humanity, had been man-made for purposes of so-called defence. No one disputed that the newspapers of the time – brittle, now, and yellow with age, but still readable if handled carefully – were full of horror stories of men's aggression.

MAN RAPES SIX-YEAR-OLD GIRL
WIDOW, 81, ATTACKED IN HER BED
WOMAN HACKED TO DEATH BY GANG OF YOUTHS

Men; always men.

Hal had heard the arguments over and over, both for and against. For the most part he chose to hold himself aloof. It had been an embarrassment ever since he could remember, having a mother who was a rebel, just as it was an embarrassment having a mother who chose to go against all the norms of society by living with a man, as if they were barbarians from olden days. Some muttered that if David and April had their way those olden days would come back again, with all the rape and violence that had been an inescapable part of them.

Hal swallowed. 'What are they going to do with me?'

'That you must ask David. Try not to take it too hard! They have your best interests at heart and I can't believe it will be for very long. When you come back, you'll be the first of a new order. It's necessary, Hal . . . someone has to lead the way. Who better than you? April will be proud of you! It means everything to her – everything she's worked for, all these years. Her and David together. Don't let them down!'

Hal stood blinking, trying to keep back the childish tears of rage and self-pity, as David struggled back up the slope. He noticed, for perhaps the first time, that David was not only not a young man any more, but not even a middle-aged one. His shoulders drooped, dispiritedly, as he reached them.

'Like sheep,' he said. 'Like lambs, in the old days, to the slaughter.'

Hal could have warned him – he *had* warned him; but as usual he hadn't listened. David had been so busy all these years fighting for a cause that he had lost touch with the way ordinary people felt. His reputation amongst the boys' community in the valley was that of a reactionary and troublemaker. He wanted to turn the clock back, they said; drag them down into the mire of pre-plague civilisation – if civilisation it could be called. The plague had taught them a lesson which ought never to be forgotten. If everyone else could see it, why not David and April?

'I'm afraid,' said Danilo, 'the young have a herd mentality.'

'They will live to regret it.' David said it heavily. He looked sad and defeated as he stood there, his hands hanging at his sides. Hal, who was accustomed to think of David as strong – almost as strong as Meta and Linden, his two most implacable opponents – felt a small surge of compassion seeping into the morass of his own self-centred misery. Danilo obviously felt something of the same.

'It may be too late to save the older ones, but the younger ones will have cause to thank you.'

'I most desperately hope so.'

'Rest assured! Hal – ' Danilo clapped him on the shoulder. 'I'll say goodbye for the moment. May you be restored to us soon!'

David had brought a second horse with him. They rode in silence out of the valley on the same journey which Hal had made two years before – and should not have been making again for another three. At last, in a tight, carefully controlled voice, he said, 'Where are you sending me?'

David flinched. 'You make it sound as though we're punishing you.'

It was the way it felt.

'I wish you could look upon it as an adventure. Both Keren and your mother would have given their right arms to go where you are going.'

'Where am I going?'

'Do you remember, a few years back, we had a visit from the Outside?'

He did remember: three strange bearded men who had not been allowed into the community but had had to camp on the outskirts and conduct negotiations at a safe distance. Some of the boys, including Hal, had gone sneaking out to look at them. The girls had been forbidden, though one or two, including Keren's daughters, had boldly disobeyed instructions and come back wide-eyed and giggling. Hal himself had been awed. He had never seen men like those before, with hair all over their faces and strange deep voices. They had seemed more wild beast than human being.

'You remember the one called Daniel? Probably not, you were too young. Daniel first stumbled upon us many years ago, when I was only about three years older than you are now.'

'When you'd just come from the Boys' House!' He was quick to get it in. David dipped his head in acknowledgement.

'When I had just come from the Boys' House – and was already beginning to question what had been done to us. It was a shock for Daniel to realise that anything *had* been done. You have to understand, Hal, that in Daniel's community the men are what you call uncivilised. To them, that is a perfectly natural state of affairs.'

'And that's where you're sending me?'

'There is nowhere else that we know of. If there are other communities, we have not discovered them. But you'll be well looked after; Daniel gave us his word. When he came to us originally he was in a pretty bad way. He'd been injured in a fall, he'd broken his arm as I remember. We patched him up and took care of him till he was fit enough to travel. He was honourable enough, last time, to say that he owed us for that. If ever the day came when we needed sanctuary for any of our young boys, he would be more than willing to give it. So . . . we're now taking him up on his offer. We've been hoping against hope we wouldn't have to, but as Danny says, it won't be for long. It's a shame none of the others has opted to go with you – '

'They wouldn't.' Hal tried to keep the contempt from his voice. How could David be so out of touch? 'Why should they want to come? Boys' days – ' his voice cracked – 'boys' days are the best days of your life!'

'But, Hal, don't you see?' David said it earnestly. 'They shouldn't be!'

There was still a smattering of people outside the Central Hall when David and Hal arrived. Several of the older members of the community, men as well as women, looked askance as they rode towards it. It was unheard-of for a fourteen-year-old boy to be brought back from the Boys' House. Hal couldn't help noticing, on the other hand, that some of the younger girls, the more daring ones, stood openly staring until dragged away by outraged elders.

'All this – ' David said it through lips which barely moved – 'is what we are seeking to change. Don't let it worry you. Daniel had worse than this to put up with.'

Hal rode on, looking straight ahead between his horse's ears, trying not to let his cheeks fire up.

'Hal!' It was April, stumbling down the steps towards him, supported by Keren. He was shocked to see how old and frail she had grown in his absence. Beside the stocky form of Keren she looked positively sparrowlike.

'Hal!' She clutched at him with a hand that was paper-thin. 'Has David told you?'

'He said you'd lost the vote.' He could have added, *again*, but she was too obviously distressed.

'Next time it will go our way! I swear it will!'

'We've got the horses all ready and waiting,' said Keren. 'We thought it best to be prepared, just in case.'

'I don't understand.' He said it stolidly, looking from one to the other of them. 'If you're so confident that next time you're going to pull it off – '

They weren't confident, of course; they were just saying it to buoy him up – to buoy themselves up.

'There can't be another vote for at least eighteen months,' said Keren. 'By then it will be too late . . . you'll be sixteen. If you're going to go at all, you've got to go now.'

'You should be ashamed of yourselves!' A new voice chimed in. It belonged to Hope, his elder sister. Unlike Keren, Hope had never rebelled against society. Her son Judah had gone through the Boys' House without any trouble, just the same as everyone else.

'You've absolutely no right to do this to him! You're making him an outcast from his own community. They can't force you, Hal. If you want to go back to the Boys' House, you have only to say so.'

He glanced uncertainly at David.

'She's right, of course.' David confirmed it, gravely. 'No one can force you. Ultimately, the choice has to be yours.'

'Oh, but Hal – ' April broke off, tears in her eyes.

'Oh, Hal, please!' she whispered. 'For my sake . . . please! We've fought so long and so hard . . . I don't think I could bear it!'

'You're being totally unfair,' said Hope. 'You're putting a quite impossible burden on him. You're just using him for your own political ends.'

'If you think,' said April, her voice tremulous, 'that it's easy for me to send my own son away – '

'You're ruining his life!' snapped Hope. 'He'll never be able to come back here!'

'Oh, I think that he will.' Meta had appeared, tall and statuesque at the top of the steps. Hal had always been in awe of Meta. She, along with Linden, was an acknowledged leader of the community. It was hard to believe that she and April were the same age, the one still so lean and lithe and upright, the other so small and shrunk. They had been the best of friends in their youth, and that, too, was hard to believe. They had been fighting on opposite sides for as long as Hal could remember.

'Sooner or later – ' Meta came gracefully down the steps towards them – 'the vote is going to go your way, and I should personally say it's going to be sooner rather than later.'

'No thanks to you!' April swung round upon her, hostility lending her a sudden spurt of energy. 'You've blocked us at every turn!'

'If it's any help,' said Meta, 'I can tell you that next time, while I shan't be voting with you, I shan't be voting against you. It's up to you. If you can manage to convince enough people, I won't oppose you.'

'A bit late in the day! A pity you couldn't come to that earlier, before – ' she stumbled – 'before – '

'April!' David caught her just in time. 'Don't, sweetheart!'

'Well, what am I supposed to do? Go down on my knees? When it's thanks to her I'm losing my son?'

'Not losing him.' David corrected her, very firmly. 'Saving him.'

'If it weren't for her, he wouldn't need saving!'

'April, be fair! We knew – ' with just the mildest of reproach, he reminded her of the fact – 'we both knew, when you opted for a son, there was a chance this might happen.'

'I know,' sobbed April. 'But I never thought it would come to it!'

The leavetaking was painful. April wept and clung to him at the same time as she entreated him to go. Her arms, at the last moment, had to be gently prised apart by Meta so that he could set his foot in the stirrup and swing himself into the saddle.

A small crowd had gathered to watch them depart – Hal, David and Keren, who were to go with him on the journey. No one in Hal's lifetime had ever left the community before; no one had ever ventured so far afield. From Croydon to the West Country, Keren reckoned, must be nearly two hundred miles.

'This is folly!' exclaimed Hope; and most people present nodded their heads and murmured agreement.

'Folly!'

Linden had arrived. She stood, arms folded,

watching with chill blue eyes as David brought up the three pack ponies that were to accompany them. Linden had always been an even more implacably hostile opponent of David and April than Meta. She was one who would never shift her ground. Her voice rang out, a brittle splinter of sound, cold and sharp as an icicle.

'Does this boy know what he is doing?'

She strode forward, coming to a halt in front of Hal.

'Has anyone told him that, once he has left us, he has left us for ever?'

'No!' The agonised cry came from April. 'Next time round we shall win the vote!'

'You will never win the vote!' Linden turned on her, quick as a whiplash despite her age. 'As long as I have breath to breathe, you will never win the vote! And if that is what you have told him – ' she grasped the bridle of Hal's horse, forcing its head down towards her – 'then you have wilfully misled him! Do not think,' she said to Hal, 'that you will ever set foot in this community again!'

They watched, in silence, as Linden stalked off. The only sound was that of April sobbing, in Meta's arms.

'Hal?' David urged his horse forward, until it was on a level with Hal's. 'You heard what Meta said earlier. You've heard Linden. The decision is yours.'

'You have no right!' screamed Hope. 'You have no right to force such a choice on a fourteen-year-old!'

'At least I'm giving him a chance. It's more than I ever had. Well, Hal? Which is it to be?'

Hal glanced from David to Hope, to Keren, to Meta, his gaze finally coming to rest on April. She held out her arms, imploring.

'Go, Hal! Go! For my sake . . . go!'

She had made his decision for him. He pressed his heels into his horse's flanks.

His last sight of the community, as he rounded the bend in the lane and turned his head to look, was of April, still weeping, as she was led away by Meta.

Chapter Two

The journey to the West Country took just over two weeks. They traced their route by an old map which Keren had found in the library, using, as far as possible, the large blue roads called motorways, which enabled them to avoid the towns.

Hal would have liked to go through a town, to see what was left of the old civilisation, but David was scared it might not be safe. Towns, in any case, said Keren, would probably by now be impassable. Even the motorway routes, though still fairly easy to distinguish, had been largely overtaken by scrub and by bramble.

It was early spring and the weather in their favour, but the going, even so, proved tough in places. Off the motorways it was frequently a case of having to hack a path through dense thickets or, when these proved impenetrable, finding a way round, which could lead them several miles off course. Then David and Keren would have earnest consultations with map and compass and anxious hours would pass before they could be certain of having re-established themselves on the right path.

Despite his trepidations, Hal could not but feel a certain awe, to think that they were treading where no human foot had trod for well over a century. The Outsiders, he knew, for David had told him, had taken a different route, sailing round the coast as far as the River Thames and up to

London, then continuing across country on foot. But that had been some years ago. London even then had been growing too hazardous to be traversed in safety. The Outsider Daniel had reported there was constant danger of being hit by falling masonry as buildings imploded or shed various parts of themselves. There were also rats, 'as large as dogs', hunting ferociously in packs amidst the rubble. A bite from a rat, said David, could precipitate a second plague every bit as deadly as the one of ninety-nine.

'It could wipe out our entire community at a blow.'

'Do you think – ' it was a question which Hal and his friends had often and animatedly discussed – 'do you think there *are* other communities?'

'Apart from us and Cornishtown? I should say it seems likely.'

Most people were agreed that there must almost certainly be other pockets of humanity which had managed to survive; the problem was to find them.

'Why haven't we ever sent out an expedition?' It was what Hal and the other boys could never understand. If there were people out there, why not go and look for them.

'It has occasionally been suggested.'

'So why haven't we ever done it?'

'Because we're too scared.' Keren said it witheringly. 'We don't know what we might find – and we don't think we want to know, thank you very much!'

'Don't forget,' said David, 'that in the early years

it was a case of simple survival. We didn't have the energy to waste sending out search parties.'

'For goodness' sake!' Keren tossed her head, impatiently. 'We've been around long enough. You'd think someone would have had the will to stir themselves and take a look. I've suggested it more than once.'

'You might say the same of any other communities that are out there. We may not have gone looking for them, but by the same token they haven't come looking for us – or if they have, they haven't found us.'

'One lot did,' said Hal.

'Yes!' Keren pounced, triumphantly. 'And you know what our reaction was? Keep away, don't come near, we don't want to know!'

'Be fair,' urged David. 'There was a reason for that. Society has good cause to fear men bearing weapons.'

'Except that they had no intention of using them, once they knew we had none.'

'You still have to ask yourself, why they were carrying them in the first place.'

'Why were they?' said Hal, interested.

David hesitated.

'Linden would tell you that it's because their men have not been civilised, and perhaps that is so, but you have to understand that their community developed along a different route from ours. They chose to carry with them much of the baggage of the twentieth century: we did away with it. We have almost a hundred and fifty years of civilisation behind us. When we finally manage to win the vote there is no danger, believe me, of our lapsing back into barbarism.'

It was what the argument was all about. Those who opposed David and April held that it was in the nature of men to be violent, and that only by civilising them could that violence be held in check. David and April had always argued passionately that it was up to society itself to contain it, to channel it positively for the benefit of humanity. But why should society have to? When violence had been unknown for over a hundred years, why run the risk of reintroducing it?

'You don't seem convinced,' said David.

'Well, but suppose people did become violent again? You don't actually *know* that it wouldn't happen; not for certain.'

'We don't know anything for certain. That's perfectly true.'

'So why do it? When it's not necessary? Why not just – ' Hal voiced his doubts tentatively, nervous of Keren's contempt. She had not David's forbearance in the face of opposition. 'Why not just leave things the way they are?'

'The simple answer,' said Keren, 'is that we need you.'

'*Me?*'

'Men: as nature made them. We need the spice – we need the challenge. Our muscles have grown flabby for want of use.'

Hal glanced at his sister in surprise. She looked anything but flabby to him, sitting stocky and upright astride her horse. David smiled.

'She doesn't mean individual muscles. She means the community's.'

'No opportunity to flex them. No cutting edge. We've developed a siege mentality . . . scared to venture forth for fear of what we might find.'

'We're venturing forth now,' said Hal.

'Yes; and you probably do fear what you might find.' David said it soberly, as if for the first time seeing events through Hal's eyes rather than his and April's.

'*Do* you fear?' said Keren.

Hal bit his lip and looked away. The honest response had to be yes. He not only feared what he might find, but feared lest Linden's words came true. What if next time, yet again, they failed to carry the vote? Next time, and the time after, and the time after that?

David reached across and gripped his wrist.

'Have faith,' he said. 'We won't let you down.'

They reached the community of Cornishtown early on the evening of the sixteenth day, approaching through a fold in the hills. They were unsure, at that point, of their exact whereabouts – 'A place on the coast, just west of Plymouth,' the Outsider Daniel had said. David had pinpointed it on the map all those years ago, never truly believing that they would have to use it. Now he and Keren stopped the horses and took out the map to debate their position, and it was Hal who saw the men coming up the valley towards them.

'Look!' He pointed. The men were dark and bearded, as he remembered them. They were carrying what he at first took to be sticks, held under the arm and pointing forward. Only as they drew nearer did he recognise them as guns.

'Keep calm,' muttered David. 'Do nothing to alarm them.'

Hal swallowed. These were the people they were going to leave him with?

The men had stopped, a short distance away. One raised his gun, in an unmistakably threatening gesture.

'Who are you? What do you want?'

David spoke calmly, in measured tones.

'My name is David. This is Keren, this is Hal. We should like, if we may, to speak with Daniel.'

The men conferred with each other.

'Does he know of you?'

'He and two others visited our community some years ago. He said, if any of our young boys ever needed sanctuary, we might come to him.'

Again, the men conferred. One of them grunted. The other, still keeping his gun levelled, moved slowly towards them.

'All right! Get down and start walking. I'll take the horses.'

They followed the first man out of the valley. Below, Hal could see a sprawl of buildings, and beyond them a vast expanse of something dark and shining. It took him several seconds to identify it as the sea.

Years later, looking back on those first disorienting days, it was this memory of the sea which remained clearest in his mind. The sea was huger than he had ever imagined it, stretching endlessly, as far as the eye could follow, jet black in the evening light, heaving and swelling on either side of a blood-red swathe carved by the sinking sun.

One thing he had not realised was that the sea was never still but in continuous movement: that the sea was never silent but murmured and swished and slapped against the harbour walls. It seemed to him like a living entity.

For the rest, he could recall very little from the general confusion of first impressions. He had a memory of stumbling down a hill between David and Keren, of being marched through a wooden gate in what seemed to be some kind of barricade, and of being led along a narrow street with buildings crowded on either side. He had a memory of people suddenly appearing from all directions, gathering in little knots to whisper and stare. He could remember it crossing his mind, somewhat bitterly, that he had been made an oddity in his own society only to be brought here to be an oddity in someone else's.

Other than that, only a few random scenes remained clear in his memory. He could remember his first sight of the Outsider Daniel, striding up the street towards them; massive – or so it seemed to the boy that Hal then was; with great slabs of solid muscle and bare, bulging biceps, like knotted ropes, carpeted in a forest of thick black hair. The same black hair hung down to his shoulders, covered the backs of his hands and the lower part of his face, even curled out of the open neck of his shirt. Was this, thought Hal, how David wished all men to be? He had felt in that moment that he could understand Linden's revulsion. What words passed between the two men, David and Daniel, he could no longer recall, if indeed at the time he had even been aware. There had been too much else to claim his attention. All that remained from their meeting was the vivid visual contrast that they made: David slight of build, beardless, grey hair cropped short, a reed beside a giant oak.

It was this impression of sheer brute strength – of all the Outsiders, not just the man Daniel – which was what had struck Hal most forcibly. The men that he knew were not like this; they had a softness about them, almost a gentleness. It was women who were the stronger sex. David, as one of the community's leaders, had always been an exception – and even David lacked the hard cutting edge of Meta and of Linden. The women in this community hung back, meekly, behind the men. Not a single woman had come forward to meet them. Such an inversion of the natural order of things had disturbed and worried him. How could he ever hope to survive in such a society, even for the short time that he had been promised?

The man Daniel had held out his hand, as if expecting Hal to place his in it. Hal had instinctively recoiled, and the man had laughed; a deep, rich, booming laugh which Hal could sense, even then, contained an element of derision.

David, mildly reproving, had said, 'To shake hands, Hal, is the custom in this community,' and reluctantly Hal had placed one of his inside Daniel's great paw. Daniel had laughed again as slowly and deliberately he closed his fingers and began to squeeze. It had been painful, but Hal had not cried out. He had known, instinctively, that the man was testing him; that even in this strange and barbarous community it was not the custom to crush a person's hand until the bones felt near to being broken.

When Daniel had at last released him, he had felt that the man had looked at him with a faint dawning of respect.

One thing he remembered, and remembered clearly: there had been no attempt to offer his hand to Keren. She had stood, ignored, a mere woman amongst the men.

He had often wondered, later, how she had felt about it; whether it had given her any pause for thought, or shaken in any degree her belief in the cause for which she was fighting.

They spent the night under Daniel's roof; he remembered that, though not the details. A few small incidents only had lodged in his memory – Daniel referring to an unsmiling, grey-haired woman as 'my wife', a word which held no meaning in Hal's vocabulary. (He had asked Keren, afterwards, and she had explained that it was a term from olden days, when men and women had paired off and lived together. 'You mean,' he had said, trying hard to understand, 'like David and April?' It had been David, with unaccustomed curtness, who had replied, 'No. Not like David and April.' But when Hal had asked what the difference was he had refused to explain. 'You will learn,' Keren had said, 'when you have been here a while.')

Other memories were of two more large, bearded men arriving and being introduced as Ansel and

Hew, and of Ansel and Hew addressing Daniel as 'Father', another word which held no meaning.

('Father is the male word for mother,' Keren had told him; but how could that be? It made no sense.)

An incident which had puzzled him at the time occurred when Daniel's wife (whose name he only discovered years later was Dorothy) went to prepare them some food. Daniel followed her out into the kitchen, and Hal heard again his uproarious laugh, tinged as before with derision.

'They'll shit themselves if you offer them that!'

It was weeks before he realised what it was she had been going to offer them.

David and Daniel sat talking, that first night. Hal could remember striving to keep awake, to listen to what they were saying, but sleep very quickly overcame him. There was only one snatch of their conversation he could recall with any clarity.

'You granted me the favour,' said Daniel, 'that first time I came to you, of allowing me to address your community.'

'I remember!' David had smiled. 'We gave you a somewhat rough ride, did we not?'

'Some of you did. That pair of she-devils – the black bitch. What was her name?'

'Meta.'

'That's right! Her and some blonde bit with eyes like chips of ice and voice like a steel blade – '

'Linden. They're both still with us. Both still implacable – well, Linden is. Oddly enough, I believe Meta may be coming round.'

'You amaze me! I feared for my manhood every time she looked at me.'

'She seems to be . . . moderating slightly in her old age.'

'Hm! If you've converted that one you must be getting somewhere. I was going to say, I'd extend the same courtesy to you as you extended to me and call the community together, but where I met hostility, I fear you might meet ridicule. I would sooner spare you that.'

Hal could remember David's reply – 'Hostility would certainly be easier to bear' – but must then have fallen asleep, for he could remember no more.

It had troubled and puzzled him for a long while, why anyone should seek to ridicule David.

The following day Keren and David took their departure, leaving Hal on his own amongst the harsh, bearded strangers whilst they went back to the ordered peace of their own community.

'Trust us,' said David. 'We shall send for you.'

Keren kissed him on both cheeks – a mark of affection rarely shown between grown women and adolescent boys.

'Be brave,' she whispered. 'Remember that when you come back to us you will be the first of a new order.'

He most desperately did not wish to be so. He would have given anything in that moment to be returning home; only the memory of April, crying out – 'Go, Hal! Go! For my sake!' – kept him from running after them.

The alien presence of Daniel at his side forbade the luxury of self-pity. He watched David and Keren, accompanied as before by two men with guns, ride out through the gate and up towards the fold in the hills. In spite of himself, a sense of desolation swept over him. As David turned in the saddle to raise a hand in farewell, tears finally filled his eyes and he wept. He wept for David and Keren, who were going without him; for April, whom he might never see again; for Andrew and Steven and all the others whom he had left behind in the Boys' House.

He was brought up short by a cuff round the head.

'You can cut that out! You've managed to escape being made into a eunuch . . . don't start behaving like one!'

Chapter Three

'I'm putting you with a family of Watchers.'

Daniel laid one of his great hands on Hal's shoulder and turned him away, not back through the gate but in a different direction, towards a wooded area running up the side of the hill.

'They're outdwellers; we tolerate them, so long as they keep themselves to themselves. You'll do better with them. There's a family, name of Marriott . . . never been blessed with a son. They could use you, I reckon. Probably better for you than staying down here with us. Your lot are a bit of a joke, to tell the truth. You mightn't like it, the things some folk'd be liable to say. You're one of the lucky ones, boy! One of the ones that got away.'

Hal didn't feel very lucky, as he obediently trudged up the hillside at Daniel's elbow.

'Why are we a joke?' he said.

'You're asking me, why you're a joke? A society of eunuchs run by women?' Daniel laughed; the old derisive laugh that he was coming to expect. 'It's enough to make a cat die!'

Hal frowned. They spoke with strange accents, these people – inuffta mek a caht doy. He was not always sure he had correctly interpreted what they were saying.

'The Watchers are a weird enough bunch, Lord knows; but your lot do take the biscuit!'

'What – ' Hal lengthened his stride in an effort to keep up. 'What are Watchers?'

'Watchers at the Shrine, they call themselves. They got religion; got it bad. A little band of 'em suddenly appeared a year or so back. Seems there'd been a split in their own community – '

'So there *are* other communities?'

'Only the one that we know of. Up north, on the coast, 'bout three weeks' journey – and, according to the Watchers, that's dying out fast. 'Tis the reason this lot took it into their heads to move on. The ones that are left, they're real loonies. This bunch here, they're what you might call mildly cracked. Personally speaking, I've no time for 'em, but they have their uses . . . keep us well supplied in women!'

Daniel chuckled; rich bubbles of appreciative laughter welling up from somewhere deep inside. Hal had never heard anyone laugh quite like that before. He found it, for some reason, disturbing.

'Well, come on, damn you!' Daniel cuffed at him. 'Split a smile! You look like a cat with a bowl of vinegar!'

Hal smiled; dutiful but uncertain.

'How old are you, boy?' said Daniel. 'Fourteen? And no idea what a woman is for, I'll be bound! Never mind, we'll change all that. Give it a year or two and you'll be roistering with the best of 'em. But one word of warning: don't mess with any of the Watchers' womenfolk. It's strictly hands off – except for the servers, of course. They're anybody's.'

Hal, increasingly uncomfortable, not sure that

he understood the implications – not sure that he wanted to – sought for some way of changing the subject.

'What about school?' he said, desperately.

'School? You can forget about school!'

'But – ' Hal stared at him, dumbfounded.

'The Watchers don't hold with too much learning; 'tis against their religion, same as most else. Besides, you can write, I suppose, and read? For what it's worth. Not a great deal, in my opinion. Writing and reading never filled a belly, nor yet did they put a roof over a person's head. The Watchers and us aren't so far apart on that one. We do the basics; just what's necessary. We don't go in for any fancy stuff.'

'You mean, you don't educate people?' Hal was shocked. 'You don't read books or learn about the past or – '

'Why should we want to learn about the past? Past is past. 'Tis the present we're concerned with.'

'But how – '

'Listen, you little prig!' Daniel gave him a shove. 'Don't think you can come here with your high-and-mighty attitudes. I know all about your lot – I had a bellyful of 'em! Preached at day and night, wasn't I? Call yourselves civilised . . . you churn my guts, you do! I remember when I was there that first time, they gave me a bunch of writing to look at. You know what they were up to? You know how they were a-wasting of their time? Writing down all about how it was a hundred years ago! How *men* – ' his lip curled upwards in a sneer – 'how *men* had been responsible for all the ills of the world. How they'd had to be stopped from doing all the terribly nasty things they'd done to women. Pah!'

Daniel turned, and spat. 'That's what I feel about your lot, if you want to know. Contempt! So anything you learnt there you can just forget about. I may not have much time for them Watchers with all their religious claptrap, but I tell you one thing: at least their men are men. And you just had better do as they bid you, boy, or I won't answer for the consequences!'

The outdwellers – about a couple of hundred people, as far as Hal could judge – had colonised an area on the edge of the woodland. Unlike the communal arrangements to which he was accustomed, they lived in small groups, men, women and children, in individual houses fashioned either from timber or from bricks salvaged from old buildings. The houses were of the most basic construction: one central room with others opening off it.

The groups who inhabited them were called 'families'. A family, generally speaking, consisted of a man, a woman and children. The man was known as 'husband', or 'father', the woman was 'wife', as well as mother. There were also 'grandmothers' and 'grandfathers', but not so many of these. The older folk, it seemed, had mostly stayed behind.

'Too set in their ways, they were . . . they thought we were wicked.'

It was Anne, the older Marriott girl, who explained it to him. She, too, spoke with a strange accent, different again from that of Cornishtown;

softer and more singsong. 'Too set in thurr ways, they wurr . . . they thowt we wurr wicked.' He found it difficult at first to understand, but soon picked up the rhythm of it and in the end almost ceased to notice.

The family to whom he had been handed over followed the general pattern of families: one man, one woman, and two children, in this case both girls. The man, when Hal first arrived, was away.

'You had better not ask where,' Daniel had said, with the familiar note of derision in his voice. 'You'll learn soon enough. It's one of the things you'll have to get used to.'

Just one of many. He found everything, to begin with, confusing, not least the question of how to address people. The man and the woman both appeared to be called by the same name, Marriott, which was also the name of the family. Daniel had referred to the woman as 'Missis Marriott' and to the man as 'Mister', but when Hal followed suit the woman shook her head and said, 'You'd best call me Mam if you're going to be one of us.'

He quickly learned that all the women were called Mam. All the women were Mam and all the men were Da. Only the children, or so it seemed to him at first, had proper names. The two Marriott girls were called Anne and Elizabeth. Anne was his own age, Elizabeth about three years younger.

Yet another of his confusions was finding himself in the company of girls, for in the normal course of events he would not have set eyes on a member of the opposite sex from the time he entered the Boys' House to the time he left it. It felt wrong; almost, in some way he could not define, improper. Mam, although indisputably a member of the opposite sex, did not engender the same anxiety. He could only suppose it was because she was old, though why that should make any difference he was unable to say. At any rate, he was not rendered scarlet and tongue-tied in front of her as for the first few days he was with the girls.

Anne was the quieter of the two, grave and gentle, with large docile eyes in a round face. She wore her hair, silvery blond, in a long plait down her back, as did all the Watcher girls. (All the mams kept their heads covered by yellow cloths so that you would never even know that they had any hair.)

The younger girl, Elizabeth, was very different from her sister. Where Anne was fair, Elizabeth was dark: where Anne's face was plump and soft, Elizabeth's was sharp and triangular. She was slight of build, tiny, almost spiderlike, with a short body and long arms and legs, which made her movements ungainly. She was not helped by the fact that she had something wrong with one of her feet, which caused her to limp quite badly. Hal thought, we would have put that right had she been one of ours, but the Watchers seemed to have none but the most basic knowledge of medicine.

He discovered this quite early on. Mam was plainly expecting to have a baby at any moment, and looking at her he thought that it must be a late-life child, as he himself had been. With the crippling shyness of the first few days finally broken down by the incessant magpie chattering of the younger girl who kept up a trill of conversation whether he responded or not, he put it to Anne as they worked together clearing a patch of land for planting.

'Do you have many late-life children? We used to, in the beginning, when we needed to repopulate, but we've mostly stopped it now.'

Anne turned her large soft eyes upon him. They seemed puzzled, and even slightly startled.

'How do you do that?'

It was his turn to be puzzled. 'Do what?'

'Stop having children.'

'You mean, late-life children?'

'*Any* children.'

'Well – ' He was thrown: no longer quite certain what they were talking about. 'If the women want one, they have one. If they don't, then they don't.'

Her cheeks grew pink, her eyes larger than ever. Too late, he remembered that the ways of this community were different from those he was used to. Their men were not civilised. They . . . arranged things in a more bestial fashion.

'All I meant – ' He stammered, embarrassed at his own gaffe. 'I just meant . . . Mam must be about the same age as April when I was born.'

'She's had forty-two summers,' said Anne.

'Forty-two?' That shook him. He had thought her to be far older. 'April was fifty-five,' he said. 'And *her* mother was sixty, so of course I never knew her.'

He picked up a chunk of rock, and slung it into the undergrowth. At the rate they were working it would take them, he reckoned, a good month to clear the ground – and then, he supposed, they would be set to planting it. And then there would be some other task. Resentfully he rammed the point of his wooden digger into the earth (for some reason, the Watchers had no proper tools) and teased it to and fro. He had still not come to terms with the fact that he was to receive no education while he was here. He found it painful even now to think of Steven and Andrew and the others in the Boys' House. By the time he arrived back he would have fallen so far behind he would have no hope of ever catching up.

'Excuse me.' Anne had come over to him and was standing timidly at his side. 'Did you . . . did you say . . . *sixty*?'

'Sixty; April's mother. When she had April. Yes.'

She was staring at him with something like horror in her eyes.

'I think I should kill myself,' she whispered.

He straightened up, pressing a hand to his aching back.

'What do you mean?'

'It's bad enough – bad enough – as it is! But to have to do it when you were old – '

'No one *has* to do it.'

'You can't mean they choose to?'

'They used to; quite often.'

'But – ' The colour rose to her cheeks. 'How?'

'How do they choose?'

'How do they . . .' Her voice trailed off. Glancing over her shoulder, as if fearful of being overheard, though there were only the two of them present, she whispered: 'How do they do it?'

'I don't know. The women see to it.'

'The women?'

'Well – yes.' Who else? They were the ones who had the children.

'Are you saying . . . the men don't force them?'

'No! How could they?' What strange ideas she had! 'It's not up to the men, is it? It's up to the women.'

'Not here!' Anne shook her head, quite violently. 'If it were up to us, do you think Mam would be in the state that she is?'

It was some while before the truth hit him: this society was so backward it had no means of determining when or how it would reproduce. It all happened quite randomly. He was appalled. It was like coming to live amongst savages.

'If they found a way of making us go on breeding – ' Anne knelt, tearing frantically at weeds and bits of scrub with her bare hands – 'they would keep us at it all our lives long.'

He digested this.

'What for? What would be the point?'

'To have as many children as possible.'

Coming as he did from a society where the norm for most women had settled at no more than two or three, it was a totally alien concept.

'Is it the same – ' he gestured with his digger – 'for them down there?'

'I should think it's even worse down there. At least our men are controlled by the Power. Down there they simply do whatever they like.'

He asked her another time, when they were toiling together on the same patch of ground. Hal digging, Anne uprooting, with Elizabeth crawling in their wake passing the topsoil through a sieve, what was this Power of which they all stood in such awe. Twice a day, morning and evening, they inexplicably fell to their knees and remained in silence for several minutes. It intrigued him, but no matter how he phrased his questions Anne proved unable to offer any rational explanation other than to say, rather lamely, that it was something 'that's always been there'.

'Great Power that was and is and ever shall be,' chanted Elizabeth.

'Is where?' said Hal.

Anne stretched out a hand, embracing the entire landscape.

'Everywhere. In the earth – in the sky – in the sea. But it gathers its strength in certain places. That's where we watch. At the Shrine. Some people think there might be other shrines scattered over the earth, but the only one we know of is our particular one.'

'There are bound to be others,' said Elizabeth.

'Not *bound* to be. Grandmam would say that's blasphemy. Some of the older Watchers,' explained Anne, 'believe that there's only the one source of Power. They get very angry and upset if you say there might be more.'

'They got *extremely* angry and upset when we left,' said Elizabeth. 'We're not allowed to see Grandmam any more. Nor Abby nor Jess nor Ria, even though they're our sisters. They say we're – what is it they say we are?'

'Waywards.'

'That's right. They say we're Waywards and that we'll reap our just rewards.'

'For leaving?'

'Yes, because they say we're bound to the Power for ever. But we're not!' Elizabeth rattled her sieve, triumphantly, scattering pebbles and clods of earth. 'We're here, and they're there, and they're all dying!'

'Lizzie, don't!' Anne sounded shocked.

'Well, but it's true, they are. That's why Mam and Da took us away.'

'Yes, and you know what Grandmam says! She says they're paying the price for our sins. If we hadn't broken the link, it would never have happened.'

'But it was happening.' Elizabeth said it calmly as she upended her sieve into a bucket. 'Mam and Da wouldn't have left if it hadn't been.'

'Grandmam says we must have been having impure thoughts. We didn't watch as we should.'

'Grandmam's old! She doesn't know what she's talking about. It wasn't anything to do with us not watching properly. I used to watch and watch till my eyes were sore. Now – ' Elizabeth piled more earth into her sieve – 'we only have to do it once in summer, so I don't mind so much. Even then,' she added, 'it's a bore.'

'Elizabeth, you mustn't! You mustn't!' Anne was visibly distressed. 'Don't you see? By talking like that you may be bringing things upon us!'

'How can I be? Just by talking?'

'If the Power is everywhere – and you do *believe* it is everywhere?'

'Y-yes. I suppose.'

'Well, then! Think of Mam,' said Anne. 'Think of what she's got to go through. And stop *saying* those things!'

Elizabeth sat back on her heels.

'All right,' she said. 'I won't say them. But how can I stop from thinking them?'

'You must,' said Anne. 'For Mam's sake!'

They might have been speaking in a different language for all the sense that any of it made to Hal.

Anne and Elizabeth, in those earliest days, were his constant and more or less his only companions. There were no other boys of his age amongst those Watchers who had 'made the journey'. There were some who were a couple or three years younger, and one or two who were slightly older, but the young ones were too young and the older ones had gone with the men – 'On a hunting trip,' said Anne. Hal did not ask what it was they were hunting.

'It's one of the things,' Daniel had said, 'that you will have to get used to.'

Mam, meanwhile, worried that he was not eating proper men's food. She promised that 'when Da comes back we'll see you all right'.

He asked Anne, curious in spite of himself, 'Do men eat different food from women?'

'Of course,' she said, sounding surprised. 'Men must have the best. They do the hardest work, so they need it.'

Labouring with the two girls over the interminable patch of ground, he could hardly convince himself that he was working any harder than they, but, 'Men are always more important,' said Elizabeth. He was never sure, with Elizabeth, whether she was mocking him or being serious. Already, at eleven years old, she had a more cynical view of life than the trusting Anne.

There was another sister, a married sister, Hanna, who came most days to sit with Mam and help with the domestic chores. Hanna was sixteen, grave and reflective, and resigned beyond her years – or so it seemed to Hal, used as he was to the carefree attitude of the girls in his own community.

'It's a pity you weren't here a while back,' said Anne. 'You could have come to Hanna's wedding.'

He knew that if he said, 'What's a wedding?' Elizabeth would burst into one of her peals of laughter – she found his ignorance a constant source of amusement – but he said it anyway. He reckoned if he were going to live amongst them, it was as well to learn their ways.

'A wedding,' said Anne, solemnly, 'is when a man takes a woman to be his wife.'

'And they go off and live together and the woman is made to have dozens and thousands of children whether she wants them or not.'

'E*liz*abeth!'

If he to Elizabeth were a source of amusement, she to her elder sister was a source of continuing anxiety.

'You ought not to talk like that!'

'Well, he asked,' said Elizabeth.

'Yes, but it's not the sort of thing – ' Anne blushed as she said it – 'it's not the sort of thing that you should discuss in front of a man.'

Elizabeth giggled. 'Hal's only a boy.'

'He will be a man one day, and you had better not let Da hear you talking to him like that or you'll get a beating! *And* you'll deserve it.'

Elizabeth stuck her tongue out. 'See if I care!'

'You'd better,' said Anne.

The day arrived when they were all hustled out of the house by Hanna and a stout red-faced woman called Mrs Humfris, and told to 'stay out till we say you can come back'.

'Mam's having the baby,' said Elizabeth. 'She and Mrs Humfris always go to each other when they have babies.'

They worked diligently all morning on their patch of ground, retiring to the shelter of the trees at midday to eat the food that Hanna brought out to them.

'Is the baby born yet?' said Elizabeth.

'Not yet, but I think it won't be long.'

Elizabeth flung a lump of cheese to one of the household cats, a large complacent male, patched in black and white, called Tom.

'Don't waste good food,' scolded Hanna. 'Cats are supposed to fend for themselves.'

'Tom can't fend,' said Elizabeth. 'He's too fat – and he's too lazy.' She glanced slyly at Hal. 'Do you know why he's fat and lazy? It's 'cause Da took his knackers off when he was a kitten. He said we'd got too many cats round here and it had got to stop. So he snipped him and it made him fat. Imagine,' said Elizabeth, breaking off another lump of cheese, 'if you'd stayed where you were they'd have done that to you. And then p'raps you'd have got fat.'

Hal felt his cheeks fire up.

'Elizabeth, don't tease,' said Hanna. 'All of us have our different ways. What's acceptable in one community may not be so in another. For Hal's people it obviously seems the right thing to do. For us, of course, it would be blasphemy.'

'And anyway, how does she know?' said Anne. 'Who told her?'

'Nobody told me.' Elizabeth held out a finger for Tom to lick. 'I heard Mam talking about it with Mrs Humfris . . . Mrs Humfris said she reckoned it might not be such a bad thing.'

'What?' Anne's eyes widened. 'To do *that* – ' she nodded at Tom, now idly grooming himself – 'to do *that* to men?'

'Yes.' Elizabeth nodded happily, as she munched on her cheese. 'Mrs Humfris said that would put paid to their nonsense.'

'What did Mam say?'

'Mam said she supposed they couldn't help it and it was only natural, but she did think things might have been arranged a bit better. And Mrs Humfris said, it sounds as if his lot – ' she jerked her thumb towards Hal – '*have* arranged it better.'

Anne turned, pale and tragic, to her elder sister. 'That's blasphemy, isn't it? To say things like that?' Her voice rose to a wail. 'Why did she say it? Why *now*?'

'It wasn't now,' said Elizabeth. 'It was then.'

Confusingly, the Watchers always referred to time past as 'then', regardless of whether it were yesterday or months ago, just as the future, be it tomorrow or a hundred years hence, was always 'to come'. He supposed it was logical if not precise.

'You ought not to have been listening,' said Anne.

'Mam shouldn't have been saying it. If Da got to hear – '

'Well, he won't!' Hanna cut in, crisply. 'Who's to tell him?'

Anne's eyes slid across to Hal.

'Hal won't say anything; will you, Hal?'

Hal shook his head. All this was women's talk. Nothing to do with him. (He couldn't understand half of it in any case.)

'I must get back.' Hanna scrambled to her feet. 'I'll call you as soon as it's over.'

Anne moved away, that afternoon, to work on her own. He could feel the tension mounting in her even though he could not account for it.

'Why is she so worried?' he asked Elizabeth.

'In case things go wrong.'

'Do things go wrong?' He reminded himself yet again that in many ways these people were primitive. To breed at random! It was almost unbelievable.

'Last time – ' Elizabeth squatted, squinting up at him in the sunshine – 'last time Mam had a baby it was born dead. That's what they told me. They buried it in the woods, the same as the others. But I think maybe it wasn't born dead at all. I think maybe something else happened. Do you want to know what I think?'

He didn't, but of course she told him: 'I think they had to get rid of it.'

Hal's blood chilled in his veins. What did the child mean, get rid of it?

'Why would they do that?' he said, trying to sound casual.

'I can't tell you,' said Elizabeth. 'Maybe there was something wrong with it. Like I've got something wrong.' She stretched out her left leg, with its crippled foot. In common with all the Watcher women, even the youngest girls, she wore a drab-coloured dress that reached to the ground. 'With me,' she said, 'it was just a little thing so they were able to keep me. But they'd already had to get rid of two others. Both of them were boys and Da was furious. I'm not supposed to know this,' she said, suddenly confidential. 'But I hear a lot more than they think. Anne won't talk about it, it upsets her.'

'Doesn't it upset you?' he said, wondering at her seeming cold-bloodedness.

'Not as much as when they kill kittens. I always used to cry when they did that. That's why Da took Tom's knackers off, so's he couldn't be a father any more. I'm sorry I laughed at you,' she added. 'I think it's quite a good idea, actually.'

'There has to be a better way,' he muttered. It was what David and April always said. (What Linden always said was, 'If there is, then you certainly haven't yet come up with it.')

Halfway through the afternoon, they noticed that Anne had disappeared.

'I bet Hanna came and called her and she didn't tell us!' Elizabeth was indignant. 'Let's go back and see.'

On the way there, they met up with the two girls,

Anne and Hanna, coming from the house. Anne looked as if she had been crying.

'What's happened?' Elizabeth ran towards them. 'Has it come? What was it? A boy or a girl?'

'It was a boy.'

'Is it dead?'

'I'm afraid so. But it didn't suffer,' Hanna said it soothingly, though more to reassure herself, it seemed to Hal, than Elizabeth. 'It died almost immediately. It didn't feel a thing, I promise you.'

'Have you buried it yet?'

'No. I'll see to it with Mrs Humfris. Why don't you two go off and have a walk or something? Anne's going to sit with Mam. I'll fetch you when it's over.'

Anne and Hanna turned back towards the house.

'See?' said Elizabeth, as soon as they were out of earshot. 'Another one they had to get rid of. There must have been something wrong with it again. Just like last time.'

A few days later, when Mam was up and about and the dead baby had been safely buried and forgotten ('We mustn't talk about it,' said Anne), the men returned from their hunting trip. That same evening, Hal was proudly offered his first 'man's meal'. He recoiled in horror at the sight of it.

'What's amiss?' said the man whom Anne and Elizabeth called Da, but who had roughly instructed Hal to call him Amyas.

'It's flesh!' said Hal.

Amyas leaned towards him, staring elaborately at the bleeding red slab on his plate.

'So what's wrong with it?'

'Only animals eat flesh!'

'We're all animals, lad, just as the Power made us.'

Hal swallowed. 'I'm sorry. I can't eat it.'

A silence fell round the table. Frightened eyes swivelled to look at Amyas. He was a large, powerful, but unshapely man, with thinning hair turned grey and wispy tufts sprouting from his chin. Hal braced himself, prepared for a blow. (Blows, he had already learnt, were routinely dealt out in this community and thought nothing of.)

'Man's food, Hal,' prompted Mam, in nervously coaxing tones.

'He's not a man!' Amyas said it scornfully. 'Nor yet never will be, if he carries on like this.'

'If a person never ate it before,' suggested Mam, 'then could be they need time to get accustomed to the notion.'

'I couldn't eat it,' said Elizabeth.

'Course you couldn't! You're not a man.'

'Nor is Hal. Da just said so.'

This time for sure there would be a blow. Hal flinched, on Elizabeth's behalf, but Elizabeth faced forward, boldly. And then Amyas's craggy face split into a rueful grin. He reached across and dug his fork into the butchered mess on Hal's plate.

'Well, we'll leave him be for now. Let him continue in his womanish ways a while longer. But you got a heap o' learning to do, lad . . . a heap!'

Chapter Four

Two years had passed since Hal had left a weeping April to grieve while he set out on the long journey westwards with David and Keren.

In the beginning, in his homesickness and growing desperation as the alien ways of the Watchers gradually revealed themselves, he had counted every day as it passed, striving to chart some landmarks in what seemed to him a sea of eternity. His greatest terror had been to lose all track of time, for the Watchers kept neither clock nor calendar, deeming both to be 'wickednesses' from the past. Since they likewise banned, or at any rate had no use for, writing materials, he had had to resort to taking a stick of charcoal and making marks on a tree trunk. He had had, moreover, to do it in secret, for time was the Power and the Power was time, and for man to usurp any part of it was blasphemy.

It had been almost inevitable that Elizabeth should be the one to catch him out. There was very little that escaped her notice.

'You're marking the days,' she said, accusingly, after he had been with them for about six weeks. 'I've been watching you. You put a new mark there every morning. If Da knew about it, he'd flog you. That's meddling with time, that is.'

'I'm not meddling with time,' he muttered. 'I'm counting it.'

'What do you want to count it for?'

'So I know how much of it there is.'

She was obviously puzzled.

'See,' he said, 'seven of these marks makes a week, and four weeks make a month and twelve months make a year.'

'And then what happens?'

'Then you – you start again. On another year.'

'What for?'

'So that you know how many have passed. So you know how *old* you are.'

'I do know how old I am! I've had eleven summers.'

'You see?' He said it triumphantly. '*You're* counting time!'

'Not like you are. Not breaking it up into little bits and pieces.'

'It comes to the same thing. It's just not as efficient. For instance, how do you know how long it's going to be before you've had *twelve* summers?'

'I'll know,' said Elizabeth, 'when it's summer again.'

'But you don't know how long you've got to *wait* for it to be summer again. And anyway, suppose you weren't born in the summer?'

'Then I'd be a winter child, like Anne. Anne's had fourteen winters. How many have you had?'

'Fourteen years and eight months,' he said.

She furrowed her brow. 'What's that mean?'

'It means – ' he used the charcoal stick to work out a sum on the ground – 'it means that I've lived 5,590 days! I wouldn't have known that if I hadn't made these marks, would I?'

'I suppose not,' she said, grudgingly. 'But I still

don't see what use it is. It doesn't seem to me it's worth getting a flogging for.'

Nor, after a while, did it seem so to him.

As the months passed and turned into years and still there was no sign from David, he had to assume that the vote had been lost yet again. David had said he would send for him when the time was right; he had given his word, and Hal trusted him. Until then, he could only resign himself to living with the Watchers and adapting to their ways, barbaric though some of them might seem.

By the end of two years, or what he reckoned to be two years – he had long since lost count of the weeks or the months, but spring, even amongst the Watchers, was still spring – he had more or less come to terms with his new existence.

He had been initiated, reluctantly, into what Mam called 'men's work', going off on extended hunting trips with Amyas and the other males of the community. It had sickened him, at first, this slaughter of living creatures; but they had jeered at him and accused him of being womanish, a term he had quickly come to recognise as an insult, and Judd, who was the brother of Mikel, who had married Hanna, took him to one side and warned him that it was going against the Power, this setting himself up to be different from the others.

Judd's logic ran thus: it was the Power who had put all animals, including man, upon the earth. It was the Power who had given man the necessary strength and cunning to hunt and kill the other animals. It therefore followed that it was the Power's design that man should do so.

Hal had learnt the folly of attempting to argue with any of the Watchers on matters concerning the Power. He had stood out for as long as he could against being fed 'man's food' until Amyas had finally lost patience and beaten him into submission.

'For your own good, lad!'

It was what David had said when he sent him away from the community. David had reasoned with him, April had pleaded. Amyas simply stripped a length of birch and thrashed him till he was raw. He could have held out, but what would have been the point? He had to live amongst these people.

Now he ate men's food without even thinking about it, just as he hunted and killed. If ever it crossed his mind to wonder how David would feel, he angrily dismissed David's feelings as irrelevant. David had chosen to leave him here, so David must accept the consequences. Did he think, after two years, that the Hal who returned to them could be the same as the Hal who had been sent away? Or – it was another thought which crossed Hal's mind, fleetingly and unbidden, but persistent all the same – had David known from the beginning that the chances of Hal ever returning were slim indeed? Linden had sworn that, as long as she had breath to breathe, they would never win the vote.

'Do not think that you will ever set foot in this community again!'

David was strong – but Linden was stronger. If

she had outflanked him yet again, if she continued to do so, might there come a time when Hal himself had no wish to return?

He made friends with Judd and Pasco, the two boys nearest him in age, and they took him down to the town, the first time he had been there since the night he had arrived with David and Keren. He discovered that the Watchers were still regarded as curiosities, and that he was regarded as one of them. The Watchers, in their turn, held themselves morally aloof, suspicious of what went on amongst the unbelievers who dwelt below. None of the Watcher womenfolk were allowed down there for fear they might be contaminated – women, as Judd explained, being easily led into wickedness. When Hal asked, 'What sort of wickedness?' Judd said, 'The sort of wickedness that makes them question the Power.' Which, added Pasco, they were naturally prone to do.

'Their minds are as weak as their bodies. They find it hard to resist temptation, even the best of them.'

'That Elizabeth.' Judd nodded, censoriously. 'She's a force for evil, I reckon.'

'Elizabeth?' Hal was startled. What had Elizabeth ever done?

'She's one that questions. I've heard her, blaspheming and uttering heresies.'

'She was marked by evil from the start.' Pasco tapped his left foot, knowingly. 'Come to a bad end, that one will. Mind, I'm surprised your Mikel was let marry into the family.'

'It's only Elizabeth. Hanna's all right.'

'You don't know that yet; too soon to say. Wait and see what happens, I would.'

Hal was disturbed when they spoke like that. He could half guess their meaning, but not the implications. Hanna, he knew, for Elizabeth had told him, was pregnant for the second time. The first time, 'something had gone wrong', the baby had been born before it should have been and had not survived. He was aware, now, of a certain level of apprehension in the Marriott household, but if anyone was talking about it they were certainly not doing so in front of him. Even Elizabeth, his usual informant – like a magpie, she collected snippets of information with which she took pleasure in regaling him – was not saying anything. He understood it was to do with Hanna.

He had learnt enough by now to know that the birth of a child, in this primitive community, was a cause not for joy and celebration but for gnawing anxiety, yet it seemed to him on this occasion there was even more tension than had attended Mam's last confinement (Mam having been lucky enough, in Anne's words, to 'escape' since then).

It struck Hal that these women lived poised on a permanent knife edge of anxiety, alternating between relief at having escaped and dread of not being able to conceive, for if it were a sin to bear deformed children it was an equal sin to bear none at all, 'since what is the point of being a woman if not to have children?'

'The only purpose we serve,' said Elizabeth, rolling her eyes.

Hal had come to accept the Watchers' ways, but

their thinking still bothered him. It remained too alien for him to grasp. When he told them, Anne and Elizabeth, about the ways of his own community, Anne would listen with a dubious frown, as if not certain she should be doing so, whilst Elizabeth, bright-eyed and eager, plied him with questions.

'What do they do, the women in your community? If they're not forced to have babies all the time, what do they do?'

'They work, like the men. Everybody does whatever they're best suited to.'

'Not just cooking and washing? I hate cooking and washing! What do they do if they're doing other things?'

'Well . . .' He thought back. 'They might be doctors, or teachers. They might look after the little ones. They might work on the land. Just anything that needs doing.'

'And what about the men? What do they do? Do they do just anything that needs doing?'

'Yes. It's the same for everybody.'

'You mean, they even look after the children?'

'If that's what they're best at.'

Elizabeth would listen for as long as he would talk; she could never have enough. In spite of Anne's frequent admonitions – 'Lizzie, hush! You shouldn't be asking things like that, it'll put bad ideas into your head' – she demanded every last detail of how Hal's society was run. When she learnt that not only the men, but also the women, could both read and write she decreed imperiously that he should teach her.

'But don't tell Anne. She'd worry. She'd say it was blasphemy.'

He worried himself as secretly, in a clearing in the woods which, Elizabeth assured him, 'No one but me knows about,' he taught her the alphabet and how to write her name. He had dwelt long enough with the Watchers to feel fairly certain that it would indeed be accounted blasphemy. For himself he didn't care, he had become hardened to the frequent beatings, dealt out indiscriminately to women and children alike – by way of correction rather than punishment, as Amyas was always quick to assure him.

'This is for your own good, lad!' How many times had those words been said to him? 'The only way to keep you on the path!'

It was for Elizabeth he worried. She was as tiny as she had ever been, scarcely coming up to his shoulder, and Amyas – for her own good – spared her nothing. He had seen the man bathed in sweat after giving her a beating, but on the one occasion when Hal had attempted to intervene he had turned on him, savagely, and thrashed him almost raw. Mam, bathing his back for him afterwards, had begged him, 'Never do such a thing again. Da feels bad enough as it is, having to correct her. But 'tis for her own sake, Hal. She must learn to obey the Power else I dread to think what will happen to her.'

Anne cried out and covered her ears when Hal said that in his society they acknowledged no Power: Elizabeth said that she should like to go there. To Judd and Pasco he never spoke of such things. Their beliefs were set and he sensed it would be unwise to challenge them. They showed, besides, little interest in any society save their own, the only questions they ever put to Hal being concerned with the ritual castration ceremony which took place after five years in the Boys' House. They marvelled that men should allow it to happen, exclaiming in a mixture of scorn and wonderment when Hal attempted to put the women's case as he had heard it so often from Linden and Meta.

'You're never saying you'd have let them do it to you and not put up a fight?'

He found it difficult to explain that he had been brought up to believe it was the natural order of things. David and April might have fought against it, but secretly he had been ashamed of David and April and their reactionary views. He had wanted only to be like the others.

'You'd have let them make a woman of you?'

'Not a woman! I'd still have been a man.'

'Call that a man?' jeered Pasco.

'No man as I know,' said Judd ''d let a parcel o' females do that to him.'

'When you're young,' pleaded Hal, 'you don't know any better.'

'Hah! But you do now,' said Judd. He closed one eye in a wink. 'You do now,' he said, 'don't you?'

Hal supposed that he did. He might not yet appreciate the full enormity of the act of civilising, as Judd and Pasco would have him do, but the Watchers would certainly appear to demonstrate without any doubt that men left in their natural state were stronger both mentally and physically than women. As Pasco had said, women's minds were as weak as their bodies. If Elizabeth were anything to go by, they did find it hard to resist temptation.

Even Mam had uttered blasphemies in her time; she and Mrs Humfris together. And what had happened to Mrs Humfris? For her sins, she had been taken back to join the dwindling sect of the Strict Watchers. He didn't know the full story, but Mam had shed tears when she had gone. Mrs Humfris had been her friend: there was no one else she dared confide her blasphemies to.

Hal supposed, rather vaguely, that if you ran a society based upon belief in a Great Power, then all members of that society should subscribe to it and obey whatever rules were laid down. If the women found the task beyond them, and it seemed that many of the Watcher women did, then it had to be up to the men to keep them in order. He could understand why Amyas found the need to beat Elizabeth, with her continued, reckless questioning, though he did think it would be better if some other means of persuasion could be found. Coming from a society where differences were solved by means of words rather than blows, he still found violence a difficult concept. Both Judd and Pasco, needless to say, derided the notion when he put it to them.

''Tis all they respond to!'

'You can't talk to them as you would a man. Their brains work differently.'

'When they work at all,' said Judd.

He and Pasco both laughed. Judd placed an arm about Hal's shoulder.

'You'll learn, when you're a bit older . . . women were put here for one reason and one reason only. If they do as they're bid and don't set themselves against us, they'll be treated according. It's ones like that Elizabeth that need guarding against. If you ask me, Amyas isn't half strict enough with her. If she were my da's, she'd be beat to a frazzle.'

Hal felt guilty, after that, at having encouraged her interest in his own society (though he was beginning less and less to think of it in such terms. He ought certainly never to have given in to her demands to be taught how to read and write.

'I don't think we ought to be doing this,' he said, one day. 'You could get into a lot of trouble.'

'I know.' She nodded. 'I could be beaten black and blue. So could you,' she added. 'Are you scared?'

'Not for myself. For you.'

'I'm willing to run the risk,' she said.

'But why?' He looked at her, gravely. 'Is it really worth it?'

'Yes! They've got books down there – do you know what books are?'

'Of course I do!' He was affronted. 'We have a whole building full of them.'

'So have they, only they don't look at theirs any more because most of them have forgotten how to read. You know that man that brought you here?'

'Daniel.'

'His sister came up once and tried to talk to us. She wanted to be friendly, but the men were here and they wouldn't let us. So I ran after her,' said Elizabeth, 'and I talked to her by myself without anyone knowing. And she told me about all these books and how no one ever looks at them. She said she'd learnt to read and write when she was young but her daughters couldn't because it's not allowed any more. Only the men can do it, and they don't always bother.'

'I still don't see,' protested Hal, 'that that's any reason for you risking a beating.'

'Maybe one day I'll get to read them – or maybe one day I'll leave here and go and live in your community. Do you think they'd let me?'

'Yes, but how could you ever hope to get there?'

'I could go with you,' she said.

'What makes you think I'm ever going to go back?'

'You might, one day.'

He shook his head; he was beginning to think that Linden had been right. He would never set foot amongst his own people again.

Hanna's time came and Mam went off to be with her. So, unusually, did Amyas.

'Why have they both gone?' said Hal. Childbirth was women's work. A low, animal function; no concern of men.

Anne and Elizabeth exchanged glances.

'You tell him,' said Anne.

Elizabeth waited until Anne had left the room.

'He wants to be there in case he has to say goodbye to her.'

Hal was bewildered. 'Why should he have to do that?'

Elizabeth fell silent. She was older by two summers since the day when they had worked together on their patch of ground, whilst Hanna and Mrs Humfris attended Mam. Her prattle was no longer so artless.

'She's not going away anywhere, is she?'

Elizabeth pursed her lips; it seemed that she had told him as much as she was going to.

Hal frowned and turned back to his workbench, where he was fashioning a pair of shoes. It was one of the skills he had learnt since coming amongst the Watchers. In his own community they still wore clothes and footwear from the old days, painstakingly garnered in the years following the plague and carefully stored ever since. They still had sufficient to last them for decades. The Watchers refused on moral grounds to touch any artefact or garment that was pre-plague. One of the first things Mam had done when he came to them was strip him of every article of clothing and burn them.

'You know Mrs Humfris?' said Elizabeth.

He raised his head, to look at her. 'Yes?'

'You know her husband made her go back and become strict again?'

'Yes.'

'Do you know why he did?'

'I thought it was because she'd been talking blasphemy.'

'But do you know how he knew she'd been talking blasphemy?'

'I – imagined somebody must have told him.'

Slowly, Elizabeth shook her head.

'So how, then?'

'If you want the truth,' said Elizabeth, 'she had

a baby without any arms or legs. That's how he knew.'

He stared at her, dumbfounded. Even apart from the sheer horror of it (he had no idea such things could happen) the logic escaped him. Such gross deformity, unknown in his own community, had presumably to be the result of their lack of selectivity in breeding. He failed to see where the blasphemy came in.

'It's obvious, isn't it?' said Elizabeth. 'At least – ' a note of disdain crept into her voice – 'it is to them.'

'Are you saying that, if something like that happened to Hanna, she'd be taken back as well?'

'If she were lucky,' said Elizabeth.

'And if she weren't?'

There was a silence.

'If she weren't?' said Hal.

Elizabeth's eyes, usually so direct, slid away, evasively.

'Mikel's family are stricter than Mrs Humfris'. They go twice a year to watch at the Shrine.'

'So?'

'So that's why I'm praying,' said Elizabeth, 'that Hanna hasn't been blaspheming.'

He laid down his tools, exasperated.

'You don't honestly believe all this?'

'It's what they say,' she muttered. 'Why else would the Power wreak vengeance if we hadn't blasphemed? Nothing ever happens to the men; only the women. So it's got to be the women's fault. Hasn't it?'

'We discussed this once before!' He shouted it at

her, angrily. 'You told me then that they didn't know what they were talking about!'

'Well, I don't think they do!' she cried. 'But what's the good of saying so? That isn't going to help Hanna!'

It was obvious, when Mam and Amyas arrived home some hours later, that the news was bad. Mam was red-eyed from weeping, Amyas grim-faced. Harshly he told Anne to 'go to your mother', and Elizabeth to take herself to bed. He then left the house, having ignored Hal totally.

The minute she heard the door close, Elizabeth was out of bed and scuttling crabwise across the floor to Mam's room. She, too, ignored Hal.

He sat, forlorn and alone in the near dark, feeling hurt and hard done by. Had he not as much right as anyone to care what happened to Hanna? She had been kind to him, and understanding, in those first confusing days. She had told Elizabeth not to tease him, sensing his embarrassment. She had accepted his word that he would not go running to Amyas with tales of Mam's blasphemy. Now she was in trouble and they were excluding him.

The door of Mam's room opened at last and the two girls came out. Anne had her arm round Elizabeth's shoulders. He could see that they had both been crying.

He started up.

'What's happened? Is Hanna all right?'

Anne turned a tear-stained face towards him.

'Hanna's gone,' she said. 'We mustn't talk about her ever again.'

Chapter Five

There came a time, after Hal had been with the Watchers for three springs and three summers, when Amyas decided he should accompany them on their annual pilgrimage to the Shrine. On the two previous occasions he had been left behind with the few old folk and the younger children. Now, said Amyas, it was time he played his part.

So long as he was not expected to become a Watcher and subscribe to their beliefs, he was happy enough to go with them. Any journey had to be an adventure and he was interested in seeing this Shrine they all paid obeisance to. He had once asked Anne to describe it to him, but to describe the Shrine in human terms would, it appeared, be yet another act of blasphemy. The young Elizabeth, as usual more forthcoming, had obligingly told him that it was 'big and black and horrible . . . I hate it!'

The older Elizabeth had learnt to be a little circumspect. Had he put the same question to her now she would most likely not have answered it, for when he asked her, at the start of their pilgrimage, 'What actually happens? What are we actually watching for?' she only tossed her head peevishly and said, 'It's no use asking me! I'm only a woman. I'm not allowed to see.'

'Not allowed to see what?'

'Whatever it is.'

'But you once said you watched and watched until your eyes were sore!'

'I did. I used to! But then we have to cover ourselves and not look.'

'All of you?'

'Just the women.'

'Why is that?'

'*I* don't know!' She said it querulously. 'Because we're women.'

'Are you telling me – ' he tried teasing her – 'that you've never risked a quick peep?'

'If I had,' retorted Elizabeth, 'you don't think I'd be stupid enough to tell you?'

There had been a time when she would have done; but since Hanna had vanished from their lives the defiant jauntiness which had so animated her as an eleven- and twelve-year-old had largely disappeared. She would never achieve Anne's mildness of character or meek acceptance of the Watchers' creed, but any doubts she now kept to herself.

Of course it was safer that way, but still he couldn't help mourning the loss of her bold spirit. He had admired the persistence with which she had demanded to be taught how to read and write even while he had deplored the risks that she was running. They no longer met in the secret clearing in the woods; had not done so since the day that Hanna's name had become an act of blasphemy. There were no more questions about Hal's community, no more fierce declarations of independence. She seemed resigned, at last, to following the same pattern of life as the other women.

In spite of his friendship with Judd and Pasco,

he missed Elizabeth's eager prattle and sharp sense of humour, for Elizabeth had been closer to him in spirit than anyone; and besides, both Judd and Pasco had recently taken wives, which inclined them to look upon Hal with a certain good-natured contempt. He was a mere lad: no fit companion for married men.

It left him somewhat on his own, especially as any close relationship between the sexes was forbidden. Mam had already told him, albeit apologetically and with a deal of embarrassment, that while of course it was 'all right to talk to the girls indoors, when Da and I are here,' he should try to avoid being alone with them outside.

'You see, it's not as if you're their real brother, Hal. If you were their real brother it would be different. But as it is, folks would talk – and besides, it could lead to wickedness.'

The relatively relaxed atmosphere at the start of the pilgrimage, as the horse-drawn wagons were being assembled and provisions loaded, was the first chance he had had to talk to Elizabeth on her own for several weeks.

'Will I be allowed to watch?' he said. 'Or will I have to cover my head, as well?'

'You'll be allowed because you're a man.'

'What would happen –' he said it banteringly, trying to bring out the old, irreverent Elizabeth (who must surely still be there, somewhere?) – 'what would happen if you cheated?'

'What do you mean?' She looked at him, haughtily. 'If I cheated?'

'If you sneaked a look when you weren't supposed to.'

'I'd be struck down,' she said.

'Who would strike you down? The Power? Or your da?'

'The Power, of course!'

'Why would it do that?'

'I told you!' She said it impatiently, refusing to join in the game. 'Because I'm a woman.'

'Doesn't the Power like women?'

'Nobody likes women,' she muttered. 'Except other women.'

'I do,' said Hal. 'I like you, and Anne, and Mam.'

'You're different. You're an outsider.'

'Still?' he said. 'After all this time?'

'Unless you become a Watcher, you'll always be an outsider.' She glanced at him, suddenly shy. 'I suppose you wouldn't ever think of becoming one?'

'I – ' He hesitated, uncertain how to reply. 'I don't want to blaspheme, but . . . I'm not a believer, you see.'

'You couldn't pretend?' There was a note of wistfulness in her voice.

He wrinkled his brow. 'Why should I?'

'You could marry Anne, if you did.'

He had never thought in terms of marriage. He had grown used to the idea, over the years, of men and women teaming up and living together in order to produce children. It no longer seemed as primitive as once it had, but for all that it had not seriously occurred to him that he would be expected to do so. Somewhere at the back of his mind, perhaps, there still lingered the thought that even yet David might send for him.

'She'll have to be married soon,' said Elizabeth. 'She's had nearly seventeen winters. That's old. And if you don't marry her she'll be given to that disgusting fat pig of a Huggett!'

It was a flash of the old Elizabeth: angry and impassioned. Hal squirmed, uncomfortably. If he were going to remain with the Watchers – and the more time that passed, the more remote seemed his chances of ever returning to the place he still thought of as home – then he knew that sooner or later he would be prevailed upon to marry. He supposed if that were the case then he would as soon marry Anne as anyone. But this blind, unfounded faith in some all-seeing Power – it went against everything he had ever been taught.

'Couldn't I marry her without becoming a Watcher?'

'No.' She shook her head, vehemently. 'Mam mightn't object, she'd do anything to try and save Anne. But Da would say it was blasphemy. He's already talking of taking us back.'

'Rather than let Anne marry Luke Huggett?'

'If she does marry him. Da thinks it's the only way to stop bad things happening. Because if they did – ' Elizabeth lowered her voice. 'Luke's like Mikel. Stricter than we are. He abides by the law.'

'You mean – ' Hal wasn't certain even now exactly what she did mean. It was something he preferred not to think about, just as he preferred not to think about Hanna. To this day no one had ever told him what had become of her. There were aspects of this society which even now froze his blood.

'I mean,' said Elizabeth, 'that if Da were as strict as Mikel, Mam wouldn't still be here. It's only because she's given him good service – and anyway, she's too old, now. It's all right when you're old. You're safe then. But Anne's got years and years to go! And if anything went wrong – Hal!' Elizabeth caught at his arm. 'Please say you'll become one of us! Please!'

'I don't see what difference it would make.' He mumbled it, ungraciously. 'Things could still go wrong.'

'Yes, but you'd give her another chance! You'd be prepared to break the law!'

'Why? If I'd become one of you? I'd have to obey the law just the same as everyone else.'

'Not everyone. There are just one or two . . . all the women know, though we're not supposed to talk about it.'

'Then you better hadn't! And stop clutching at me!' He shook her off, irritably. 'If anyone sees us, we'll be in trouble.'

He was sorry, afterwards, that he had been rough with her. The truth was that he had felt under pressure, and a level of panic had set in. Even after three summers he was not sufficiently committed to the Watchers to embrace their way of life in its entirety. On the other hand, the thought of Anne – sweet, patient, loving Anne – being handed over as a chattel to Luke Huggett, slack-lipped and sweaty in all his religious fervour, was distasteful enough to be upsetting and to nibble at the edges of his conscience. Marriage would assuredly be forced upon him in the not too distant future, and there was no reason, he supposed, why he could not at least learn to pay lip-service to all their mumbo-jumbo, mindless though it was. It would be no more than Elizabeth had done.

The journey to the Shrine, although conducted at a quicker pace than the one Hal had undertaken with David and Keren, for the way of the pilgrims was well marked, nevertheless took twenty-one days. Hal still retained his old habit of counting time, though it was not as compulsive as it had been. When he had asked, as the pilgrimage set out, 'How long will it take?' he had met either with frowns, at his implied blasphemy, or with the indifference of shrugged shoulders. The journey would take as long as it took. They knew when they must leave in order to arrive when they had to arrive, for at one point in the year, and at one point only, the sun fell where they had laid a marker for it to fall: that was the sign to be up and off, and was as much as they needed. (He forebore to point out that their sun-marker was simply a primitive form of clock and therefore, in their terms, just as much of a blasphemy. They were riddled with contradictions, but he had learnt to hold his tongue.)

As they journeyed ever further northwards, Hal noticed that the landscape about them was slowly changing, almost imperceptibly at first – bare patches of earth, stunted trees with strange growths such as he had never seen before – but quite soon becoming too marked to ignore. Vast plains of barren land, dark and desolate, stretched away before and to both sides of them, the withered stumps of trees, with their twisted branches bare of all foliage, the only signs that once things had grown there.

'What is it?' he whispered to Amyas.

'The beginning of the end. Our goal is within reach.'

'But – ' Hal stared about him, as the wagons moved on across the blackened earth. 'Why is it like this?'

'What you're seeing here – ' Amyas nodded at the stark horizon – 'is the manifestation of the Great Power. In its justifiable wrath it devastates all that lies about it.'

'And beyond,' said Elizabeth.

'And beyond. It knows no bounds.'

'But it's devastating more each year.' Anne suggested it, nervously. 'Doesn't it seem so to you?'

'Given the wickedness amongst us – ' Amyas, imperturbable, slapped the reins over the horse's rump – 'who should be surprised?'

Hal became increasingly uneasy as the journey progressed even deeper into the heart of the dead land. Struggling to make sense of it, he could make none. Religious belief was superstition; even David and Linden had agreed upon that. All the upbringing of his first fourteen years told him that such wide-scale destruction could only be man-made. Men, routinely, had bombed and killed before finally releasing the plague which had almost wiped life off the face of the earth. Was it starting all over again?

He asked Pasco, 'Are there other communities

that you know of?' But Pasco said no, only the Strict Watchers further east. When, originally, the Waywards had packed their bags and left the area, they had imagined that sooner or later they would come across some other community they could link up with, but they had travelled all the way to the West Country before they had stumbled on any – and then had not particularly liked what they had found. (It had not occurred to them, apparently, that other communities might fail to acknowledge the omniscience of the Power. Hal gathered it had been a rude shock.)

In the past, Pasco said, they had explored a fair distance inland without detecting any signs of human habitation, though it was true they had not ventured across the sea because to go upon the sea would be blasphemy. The Watchers' lives were hedged about with blasphemies. Many, such as measuring time, seemed to Hal both obscure in origin and meaningless as to purpose. Others, such as going on the sea, were more easily explained. People that had been upon the sea, said Pasco, had been observed to develop mysterious illnesses and die; therefore they had learnt that the sea was forbidden them. The men of Cornishtown might go upon it with impunity only because they were infidels and thus not subject to the Great Power.

'But don't you worry,' said Pasco. 'When the time comes, they'll get their just deserts.'

On the twenty-first day, shortly after sunset, they reached their destination. Ahead of them stretched the same bare and blackened earth; but in the distance, rising stark against the skyline, were what looked to Hal like a cluster of enormous pillars.

'The Power,' said Amyas, and fell to his knees.

All the rest of the party followed suit; so, after a few seconds, did Hal, since it was clearly expected of him.

Away to the right were another, larger group of people, dressed in long robes, all standing facing in the direction of the pillars. One or two heads turned, surreptitiously, towards the newcomers, then silently turned back again. Hal guessed they must be the stricter brethren from inland.

After a few seconds on their knees, the Watchers rose and clad themselves in robes similar to the ones the rival group were wearing. Mam handed one to Hal, and obediently he pulled it round him.

In both groups, he noticed, the women were ranged at the front – where the men, presumably, could keep an eye on them and make sure they obeyed the rituals. He remembered what Elizabeth had said about having to cover her eyes and not see.

The covering part of the ceremony had evidently not yet arrived. All the Watchers stood, in their separate groups, mesmerically staring ahead at the pillars. For a while Hal stared with them, but he quickly grew bored waiting for something to happen. At what point did the fun begin?

He gazed round at the assembled company, trying to catch someone in an ignoble act such as bum-scratching or nose-picking, but not a soul moved. It was as if they were made of stone. Even the slow turning of Hal's head to left and to right seemed a sort of violation.

After a bit, for want of anything better to occupy himself with, he fell to speculating on the origins of the pillars. History had never been his strongest subject, despite the fact that knowledge of the past was much prized in the Croydon community, but he seemed to recall once being shown a picture of such pillars in a book. He wondered if perhaps they had been part of one of the buildings they called churches, or cathedrals, where in pre-plague days they had gathered to worship their gods just as the Watchers now worshipped the Power. That would make sense, he thought. The Watchers, even with their almost total, and wilful, ignorance, might nonetheless have recognised a place of worship when they saw one. It must have seemed like a good idea to take it over and install their own version of a deity.

Satisfied that he had solved the mystery, Hal devoted his energies to devising ways of helping the time pass. First he counted up to a hundred with his weight on one leg, then on the other. Then he linked his hands before him and counted to another hundred, and then another with them linked behind. Another with his right fist clenched, another with his left. The permutations were numerous enough to occupy him for a good part of the night. Mouth open, mouth closed: head bent, head upright: eyes to the right, eyes to the left. It kept him awake but did nothing, in the end, to alleviate the tedium or the ache in his limbs from constant standing. The worst of it was, he had no idea when it was likely to end.

The vigil lasted throughout the night, and all the time he was conscious of the fact that he, and he alone, was exhibiting any signs of life. Even Elizabeth, whose slight figure he could make out amongst the women, stood rigidly to attention. He marvelled at her willpower, for Elizabeth, despite her crippled foot, was like quicksilver, all over the place.

Hal himself was beginning rather desperately to wonder how much longer he could subdue the impulse to start screaming, or leaping up and down, when a ripple of movement began amongst the Watchers and the breath of a sigh ran through the assembled ranks.

The first faint flush of dawn was seeping into the sky, sending flares of pink and rose streaking through the darkness. As Hal watched, the sun itself slipped over the horizon, a deep orange semicircle blazing across the blackened land. With one accord, the women sank to their knees, pulling their hoods down about their eyes, whilst at the same time the men flung back their heads and raised their arms to greet the coming of the Power. (Hal, feeling foolish, did likewise.)

A strange, guttural chanting began, growing in intensity as the sun rose higher. For a short space of time it hung there, between the columns, shining directly upon the face of the worshippers. The chanting at this point changed to a harsh, barking kind of ecstasy, gradually dying away into a series of yelps and moans as the sun severed contact with the columns and moved up and outwards on its journey across the sky.

Then the hunched figures of the women took over, beating the ground with their foreheads and setting up a low, tuneless wailing, each in unison with the others. Some of the men, unable to contain themselves, broke ranks and went staggering forward, sobbing and crying out, towards the distant columns.

Judd, who had been standing next to Hal, was one of them. It was this which shook Hal almost more than anything. That someone normally so in command of himself should fall prey to such self-abasing madness served only to confirm, as perhaps nothing else could have done, his belief that religion was folly. Before, he might have wavered. Now, he knew for certain: he wanted no part of it.

When at wearyingly long last the wailing ceased and the over-fervent returned to the ranks, something like sanity once again prevailed. The majority of the Strict Watchers, without so much as a backward glance at their co-worshippers, moved off (Hal strained his eyes in vain for signs of anyone who might possibly be Hanna) and the Waywards settled down to the prosaic business of feeding themselves. If there was no communication between the two camps, there was, at least, a certain amount of traffic as one family of Waywards peeled off to rejoin their stricter brethren and several renegades came struggling over to ally themselves with the breakaway group.

'More than usual,' hissed Elizabeth, in Hal's ear. 'Why is that, do you suppose?'

'Too many bad things happening. They're growing scared.'

'I'd be pretty scared, living near that.' He jerked his head at the Shrine, a sinister artefact in the dead landscape. 'Wouldn't you?'

Elizabeth pursed her lips. 'We may have no choice.'

Her meaning was clear enough: it all depended on Hal. He could save them if he would – or abandon them to their fate.

He thought angrily, 'Why should I be made to feel guilty?' He had been abandoned to his fate; little any of them had cared about that.

He lay down thankfully enough to catch up on some rest before they started on the long homeward journey but found himself, irritatingly, unable to sleep. Thoughts tumbled and swirled inside his head. History lessons with Danilo – Social Life before the Plague – Religious Worship – shiny coloured pictures ('photographs') of the great buildings they had called cathedrals – massive in size, but with long frail spires reaching into the sky, not in the least like the vast pillars of the Watchers' Shrine. And yet he felt certain that he had seen pictures of it, or of something very like.

He cast his mind back to other lessons – Social Organisation – Methods of Agriculture – Political Philosophy. Suddenly, he had it: Energy Sources! There had been many energy sources before the plague, some of which Danilo had been able to explain, some of which he had confessed to being baffled by. Nuclear energy was one of the ones that had baffled him.

'This was an advanced form of power about which we understand very little. What we can say with certainty is that it had a potential for destruction on a scale never known before in the course of human history. It was stored in constructions called *power stations* – make a note of that – positioned at strategic points about the globe. We believe there were several of these power stations in this country alone. We also believe they must still be there, though we have not yet come across one.

'Some people have put forward the theory that the energy stored in these power stations is still capable of being unleashed, and that they therefore represent a possible source of danger for future generations. This, however, I must stress, remains only a theory.

'One thing we do know is that leaks of what was called *radioactivity* – write that down – were responsible for a wide variety of human ills, including severe birth defects and damage to the bone marrow.

'Unfortunately, the only books which we have been able to discover that deal with the subject are largely incomprehensible given the present state of our knowledge, but we do have a few pictures which will give you an idea of what the power stations looked like . . . hardly an adornment to the landscape, I think you will agree.'

And then Danilo had passed round the pictures, and they had been pictures, he now realised, of the Shrine – or at any rate of *a* shrine.

Relief flooded through him. He thought, I will

tell Amyas as soon as we get home. Amyas would instantly perceive the futility of the Watchers' beliefs, and indeed the dangers inherent in them, and all would be well.

A sense of peace stole over him. His conscience might rest easy. Anne would be saved from her fate without any impossible demands being made upon Hal.

Come the next day, caution counselled a somewhat different course of action. Amyas was old, and set in his ways; might it not be better, in the first instance, to approach Anne?

It was a question, as usual, of getting her on her own. They were within sight of the West Country before he managed to do so. He then put it to her, earnestly, that far from being divine the Shrine was a man-made artefact which could well be housing an accumulation of power which would spell disaster were it ever to be released – to all of which assertions she blithely agreed.

'We know it was man-made. It was built for that purpose – to house the Power. We've always known that.'

'But have you any idea how destructive that power could be?'

Danilo had hinted it might even have the potential to destroy the planet. He put the suggestion to her. Once again, she readily agreed.

'This is why we have to watch.'

He stared at her, nonplussed. 'What good will watching do?'

'We watch for the signs.'

'What signs?'

'Signs that show whether the Power is displeased.'

'Displeased? How can it be displeased? It's not a person!'

'Of course not.'

'So how can it be displeased? Just a bunch of matter?'

She regarded him, gravely. 'Isn't that all any of us are?'

'Yes.' His tone was irritable. She exasperated him at times with her bland assumptions. 'But we happen to be living beings!'

'Are you saying the Power doesn't have life?'

He rolled his eyes. 'I suppose that would be blasphemy?'

'It would be silly.' Anne said it reprovingly. 'We know that It has life. It may not be life in any form that we can understand – ' She paused. 'Or are you trying to tell me that you do?'

That assuredly would be blasphemy – and not even true. He didn't understand. No one understood. It was one of the greatest mysteries bequeathed by the twentieth century.

'Look, all I'm saying,' he said, 'all I'm saying is that – these bad things that keep happening . . . has it never occurred to you that it's something to do with the Shrine?'

It was believed, Danilo had said, that land near nuclear power stations might in some way be contaminated and that to live too close was to invite problems. He had been hazy about the details, but there were articles in old newspapers and medical journals which people had studied.

'All that dead land,' said Hal. 'What do you think's causing it? It's got to be the Power!'

'We know that,' said Anne.

He thought, if she says that again I shall shake her. She looked at him, searchingly.

'What is it you're really trying to tell me?'

'What I'm really trying to tell you is that it's mindless imbecility to keep going there and gazing like a load of silly sheep! It's even more mindless actually to *live* near the thing. You'd think you'd have learnt your lesson by now . . . you're bringing all these troubles on yourselves!'

Anne gazed at him, tragically.

'By our wickedness,' she said. 'Oh, Hal, do you think we don't know?'

'Then why go on doing it?'

Slowly and sadly, she shook her head.

'You're not a believer,' she said. 'If you were, you couldn't ask such a question.'

'But for – '

'Please!' She covered her ears. 'Please, Hal, don't!'

For a while after that his impatience was such that he felt he scarcely cared any more what became of her. People who were that determinedly moronic deserved whatever fate had in store for them.

He was in this frame of mind – angry and contemptuous – when Amyas, after they had been back a few days, turned both Anne and Elizabeth out of the house and informed Hal that 'I want a few words with you, lad.' He knew what was coming, and was prepared for it.

'I'm sorry,' he said. He tried not to look at Mam

as he spoke. The anguish in her eyes reminded him of April, all those years ago. 'Please don't ask me to become a Watcher. I can't see things the way you do. I suppose – ' he had no wish to give offence – 'I suppose it's because I haven't been brought up to it.'

'You've had three summers with us, lad! Isn't that long enough?'

Hal was silent.

'What does it mean, you can't see things the way we do? You've been to the Shrine – you've watched. You've witnessed! What more do you need?'

'I can't – believe – what you believe.'

'For what reason?'

'Because I know – ' Hal said it desperately – 'from what I've read in books' (not strictly true: it was what Danilo had read) 'I know that whatever the Power is, it was made by man.'

Of course it was blasphemy; the ultimate blasphemy. It was probably inevitable that from that point on the discussion should degenerate into a furious exchange.

'It takes two to make a child!' Hal found himself shouting it, furiously. 'You can't just blame the woman!'

'And if men were equally to blame,' thundered Amyas, 'don't you think that men would be equally punished?'

'It's not a question of punishment! No one's done anything wrong. It's living near that – that thing! It's that that's done it! If you'd bothered to learn how to read, and learnt a bit about the past, you'd know that what I'm saying is right, instead of closing your eyes to the truth and putting all your faith in this – this make-believe!'

'Blasphemy! *Blasphemy! BLASPHEMY!*

With each cry of the word, Amyas hit Hal across the side of the head. Hal stood there, stolidly, taking it.

'Just tell me one thing,' he said. 'What happened to Hanna?'

Mam made a choking sound and put a hand to her mouth. Amyas's face grew mottled.

'I know no one called by that name.'

'No?' shouted Hal. 'Well, I do! She was someone kind and good and gentle who did nothing wrong except have a deformed baby caused by you – you!' He flung out a hand, pointing his finger at Amyas. 'You and the other men! Forcing her to go and gaze on that obscenity! It's you that's caused all this misery! You and your mindless beliefs!'

Amyas breathed deeply. He took a step forward.

'Get out of my house,' he said. 'Now! And don't ever dare to come back. If I catch you setting foot anywhere near here again, I'll flay the hide off you!'

Chapter Six

'Is this the first time you've ever been with a girl?'

'I – ' Hal hesitated, not wishing to make a fool of himself. 'How do you mean?' He threw it back at her. 'Been with a girl?'

Esta's eyes, blue-green like the sea with the sun on it, laughed up at him and he knew that he was being teased. She was always teasing him, just as Elizabeth had done in his early days with the Watchers. The difference was that Elizabeth had been little and spindly and eleven years old. Esta was brown-skinned and lithe and only a year younger than himself.

'I reckon you've got to be new at it!' she said. 'You wouldn't blush like that if you weren't!'

He blushed even more. He was still trying to come to terms with the fact that the girls of Cornishtown enjoyed a freedom which to the Watchers would have seemed little short of blasphemous. Even Hal, with his origins in a society where woman called the tune, was sufficiently imbued with the Watchers' way to find it, initially at any rate, somewhat disconcerting.

On the day that Amyas had ordered him from the house, he had gone down the hill to the town and sought shelter with the only person he knew.

'So you've fallen foul of them at last?' Daniel had laughed – almost appreciatively, as it seemed to Hal. A strong deep chuckle from the pit of his stomach. Apart from his hair having started to grey, Daniel had shown few other signs of increasing age. He was still the broad, muscular bull of a man whom Hal remembered.

'What was it? A woman, I suppose. I warned you, didn't I? Keep your hands to yourself!'

Hal had protested, red-faced, that it had had nothing to do with a woman; rather, it had been a question of religion.

'They wanted me to become one of them, only – '

'It stuck in your craw? Well, I can't say as I blame you for that. I couldn't stomach it myself. You'd better come in, while we think what to do with you.'

There had been a family consultation and it had been decided that Hal might as well stay with Daniel and Dorothy.

'Pa's getting on a bit,' said Ansel. 'He could do with a helping hand.'

Ansel was the only one of Daniel's sons still alive. There had been three others, including Hew, who had been there the night Hal had arrived with David and Keren. All three, said Ansel, had been lost at sea.

Why did they go to sea, wondered Hal, if it were so dangerous? He remembered what Pasco had said: one of these days they'll get their just deserts. He wondered uncomfortably if there could be anything in it.

He discovered fairly quickly why they ran the risks they did. They went to sea for fish, and if he were expecting to be clothed and fed then it would be one of his duties to go with them.

'But can he swim?' wondered Esta. 'He'll drown if he can't swim. I'd better teach him!'

It seemed to Hal that people drowned whether they could swim or not, but he was by no means averse to being taught by her – though it had greatly embarrassed him, the first time, when she had stripped down to her shift and ordered him to 'take your clothes off, then! Go on! Can't swim with your clothes on, can you?' He had retained his undergarments but still felt shy and awkward. Belatedly he had realised that in all his years with the Watchers he had never seen a woman's legs – had certainly never undressed himself in a woman's presence. Esta had only giggled and told him not to be prudish.

She was Ansel's daughter and had an older brother, Felip, who claimed to have seen Hal in town with 'two of those milksops from up there . . . I bet they didn't show you half what went on! You wait, we'll have a good time, you and me.' He closed one eye and tapped the side of his nose. 'I'll show you what's what!'

It had been summer when Hal arrived: now it was autumn. He had learnt to swim, thanks to Esta, and he had been on a couple of fishing trips with Ansel and Felip and had acquitted himself not too badly.

'He'll do,' had said Ansel; and those two words had seemed to Hal amongst the sweetest he had ever heard. He found that he very much wanted to 'do': to fit in at last and be part of a community.

Slowly he was learning yet another set of rules, adapting himself to yet another perceived morality.

There was no religion to worry about, no blasphemies continually pulling him up short, but the ways of the women were strange and puzzling.

At first he had thought their status no different from that of the Watcher womenfolk, for they had no voice on the ruling Council, no say in the way affairs were organised, and were there, so far as he could see, purely and simply to serve the men. But then he started noticing small but subtle differences, particularly amongst the younger women.

While Dorothy, for example, was dutifully subservient in all things to Daniel, never daring to question, never once raising her voice nor expressing displeasure, Esta would quite cheerfully speak her mind, even if she did receive a clout round the ear for doing so. Not that the clout carried anything like the weight of Amyas's brutal blows to Elizabeth. It seemed to Hal more like a gesture, and a fairly half-hearted one at that.

He noticed also – could hardly help but notice – that boys and girls walked the streets quite openly together, often hand in hand or even with their arms about one another. It had shocked him to begin with, steeped as he was in the Watchers' notions of what constituted wickedness. When Esta had offered to teach him how to swim, he had winced, fully expecting a hand to fly out and slap her down for blasphemy. When it had not done so he had learnt that the women of Cornishtown, though still inferior, were at least regarded as sufficiently responsible to enjoy a degree of independence denied their sisters up the hill.

Trying to work out the rationale for this, he

decided it must be something to do with their not having any religion. Religion imposed a code of morals which women were evidently not strong enough to keep unless maintained under constant supervision. Reflecting on the lives led by Anne and Elizabeth, he thought that the women of Cornishtown scarcely knew how lucky they were.

'I suppose, up there – ' Esta rolled her eyes, exaggeratedly – 'they'd say this was blasphemy? You and me being together?'

He acknowledged the fact. They were lying side by side, Esta on her back, Hal on his front, in one of the many caves which were to be found along the shoreline. Esta scooped up a handful of sand and let it trickle slowly through her fingers. Thoughtfully, watching it as it trickled, she said: 'What would they do if they caught you?'

'I don't know. No one ever did it.'

'Didn't anyone ever do anything they oughtn't?'

He thought back. 'Not really,' he said. 'Only in their minds.'

'How could you know they were doing it if it was only in their minds?'

'Because of the things that happened . . . bad things. And then they knew that the person they'd happened to had been having blasphemous thoughts. I should imagine,' said Hal, stroking a tentative finger down the side of her neck and letting it linger for a delicious moment on her breast, 'that if I went back there now I'd be having blasphemous thoughts all the time.'

She caught at his hand, holding it where it was, preventing him exploring any further.

'You never did this sort of thing before?'

'How could I?'

Even if he had wanted to, who was there to have done it with? Anne was too fixed in her beliefs, Elizabeth would simply have thought it silly. At least, he assumed that she would. It was impossible to be sure, when the subject had never cropped up. But in any case, he had never been troubled by those urges which Esta roused in him. In relation to Anne and Elizabeth it had never even crossed his mind, and since they were the only two girls he had ever been permitted to speak to he had experienced no difficulty in keeping within bounds.

It seemed suddenly, with Esta, that he was decidedly out of bounds.

'Hal!' She slapped at his hand, quite hard. 'Stop doing that!'

He was hurt. What had he done that was wrong?

'I'll forgive you this time,' grumbled Esta, 'because you're ignorant and don't know any better. But just don't do it again!'

He learnt then that this new game also had its rules. It wasn't as simple as he had thought. Touching might be allowed, but only within limits.

'Some girls might let you go further,' said Esta, severely, 'but I'm not one of them.'

Trying to joke, to restore his confidence, he said, 'How am I supposed to know which sort of girl is which?'

'If a girl lets you touch her like that,' said Esta, 'then she's the sort of girl that will let you do anything.'

'So I just have to do *that* – ' she slapped at him – 'and I'll know?'

'Yes, except if you did that to any other girl and I got to hear of it – '

'What? What would happen?'

'Do you really want to know?' said Esta. Her eyes danced, wickedly. 'I'd get a knife and I'd give you the chop! Then you'd be like all those softy men in your community where you came from!'

Even now, when he had been amongst them for four months and had proved himself, or so he thought, by going upon the sea, the folk of Cornishtown persisted in looking upon him as an object of curiosity. They were not quite sure, it seemed, whether he was a full man or only a half one. It would be better, Felip assured him, when his beard started to show, but unfortunately Hal was both fair of hair and fair of skin. He envied Felip his dark stubble.

'Is it a rule in your community – ' Hal raised himself to a sitting position, genuinely anxious to know the answer – 'is it a rule that a man only goes with one girl at a time?'

She pouted. 'It's not a *rule*. But it wouldn't be very nice, would it? Not if we're going to be a couple.' She peeped up at him from her under lashes. '*Are* we going to be a couple?'

'Why not?' said Hal. He wasn't quite sure what it entailed, but if it meant enjoying a kiss and a cuddle he was perfectly agreeable.

Felip came up to him, later that day. He wore a sly grin on his face.

'I hear you and Esta are hitting it off.'

'It seems we're going to be a couple,' said Hal.

'She doesn't let the grass grow under her feet, that one. You want to watch your step . . . she'll have you hooked before you know it!'

'Hooked?' Hal must have looked puzzled.

'Hooked – like a fish! Caught and landed. You'll be a married man this time next year, if you're not careful.'

They were back at marriage again. For just a second a vision of Anne flitted across his brain and then was gone. Anne had been determinedly stupid. He had tried to warn her, and she had refused to listen. There was nothing he could do for her.

'You'd like that, would you?' Felip nudged him in the ribs with his elbow. 'Married man, get as much as you want!'

Hal grinned, but only because Felip was grinning.

'Get on!' said Felip. 'You don't even know what I'm talking about, do you? Haven't the faintest idea! You're as innocent as a new-born babe, you are. We'll have to do something about that. Remind me . . . I'm going to have to give you a few lessons. Can't have you marrying our Esta in a state of ignorance.'

'If I did marry Esta –' he blurted it out, embarrassed as so often by these constant references which he only half understood – 'what would happen if I ever went back home? Would she want to come with me?'

'Back home? You're not going back home!'

He probably wasn't, but even now he nurtured a faint wisp of belief that David would one day send for him.

'You'd best put that right out your mind,' said Felip. "'Cause I can tell you here and now, you wouldn't be let go.'

'How do you mean, I wouldn't be let go? Who would stop me?'

'Council. They'd never give you permission. We need all the men we can. Need to be strong. Defend ourselves.'

Hal was baffled. 'Against what?'

Felip shrugged. 'Who knows? Anything that's out there.'

'You think there *is* anything out there?'

'Well, there's your lot for a start. Then them Watchers – they're all crackpots. I wouldn't trust them further than I could spit. Could be others, waiting their opportunity. We don't know, do we? Got to be prepared. So you can forget about going back home. You're one of us now, whether you like it or not.'

In fact the thought of never going back to his own community bothered him less, at that moment, than the thought that he would be actively prevented from doing so should he wish. He wondered if Daniel had ever had any intention of letting him return, or whether he had always planned on keeping him here – in which case it would mean that he had lied to David and April. Or that David and April had simply taken it for granted that he would be free to return whenever they chose to send for him. It would be typical of those two, he thought. Typical of the entire community. He perceived them now as being unworldly and naive, living in their cosy, ordered society; not an idea in their heads that other people might arrange things differently.

That night he said to Daniel, 'You know that time you came to our community after you'd been there before?'

'Second time.' Daniel nodded.

'How did you know how to find us again?'

'Marked it on the map, didn't I?' Daniel said it triumphantly. 'Want to see?'

He went to a cupboard with two drawers at the top. From one of the drawers he pulled out a small bundle of books and papers tied with a length of ribbon.

'Family possessions, these are. This old book here, this was a diary kept by my great-grandmother at the time of the plague. "*This is the journal of me, Frances Latimer*".' Daniel ran his finger along the words as he read them. 'And this other one, this is even older . . . this was written before the plague, when she was living just near to where your people are. It's got her address on it, see? "*10 Raglan Court, South Croydon, Surrey*".'

Hal leaned forward to look. The writing was round and childlike and difficult to decipher, being faded with age, but he was relieved to discover that the written word still made sense to him. Sometimes even now he would take a stick and write words in the sand, just to reassure himself that he had not lost the skill.

'That's where I headed, to find where my great-gran had lived before the plague. And do you know how I found it? I used the *A-Z!*' Daniel sat back with an air of pride. 'I don't expect you know what an *A-Z* is, do you?'

Hal shook his head.

'Shows all the streets as ever was.' Daniel placed an ancient, tattered, well-thumbed book upon the table in front of him. 'Here at the back it gives all the names. What you do, you look up the name you want, then you turn to the page it gives – ' With a flourish, he flipped back the pages, opening them at some kind of map.

'Now, see that red line? That's the line I drew to show me which path to take when I got there. And this line here . . .' he traced with stubby forefinger along a maze of what Hal took to be olden-days streets. 'This one shows your folk. See? My great-gran lived here . . . and your folk settled 'bout there. I can't properly read what it says now, but – '

Hal craned closed. The print was tiny, but he could just make out the name: Croydon.

'So that's how you found us?'

'Second time was how I found you. First time – ' Daniel settled back, reminiscently, in his chair. 'First time it might be more correct to say that you found me.'

'And you got there by sailing round the coast?'

'I did.'

'And then what did you do? Left the boat and went on foot?'

'Right through London; both times. Except that the first time it was just me on my own. Second time I had companions and I make no bones about it, I was mighty glad of them.'

'Was it scary?' said Hal.

'Dangerous, more, I'd say.'

'Would you do it again?'

'Not at my age. I've done all the journeying I'm ever like to do.'

'But it could be done?'

'Most anything can be done,' said Daniel, 'if a man puts his mind to it. Howsoever – ' He closed the *A-Z* and slapped it back on top of the diaries. 'You needn't go taking ideas into your head. I had to seek clearance of the Council before I was allowed to set out. It'd be no use your seeking it because I can tell you here and now we wouldn't give it.'

Hal thought, if I wanted to go, I wouldn't bother seeking clearance, I would just go. But in fact he had no desire to go; the Cornish community suited him very well. He was even doubtful, now, in the event of David ever sending for him, and of Daniel and the Council giving him permission to leave, whether he could actually bring himself to do so. There was too much here that he enjoyed – not least the belated discovery of what it meant to be a man. Felip had hinted there might be other pleasures in store for him yet. If so, he would have to be some kind of a fool to give it all up for the sterile existence of life in his own community.

Daniel, as if reading his mind, said: 'You know what they'd do to you if you went back there, don't you? No more fun and games for you, my lad! A quick snip and that'd be the end of your love life. Blight your prospects with that girl of yours.'

Hal flushed. 'Esta and I,' he said, 'have never done anything we oughtn't.'

'I should hope you haven't! You'd be in trouble if you had.'

'I know she's not that sort of girl.' Hal said it earnestly, anxious to prove that he had learnt the rules and was abiding by them.

'That's right,' said Daniel. 'What do you think we have servers for?'

Hal must have looked blank.

'Never tell me you've not made use of them?' Daniel laughed so much his belly shook. 'You must be feeling proper frustrated! You go to Felip. Tell him I said it's about time he got you broken in. He'll look after you. He'll see you all right. Then you come back here and tell me if you want to leave us!'

Felip, chuckling, said, 'A visit to the servers, eh? I reckon it's about due!'

'You do?' said Hal: and then, playing for time (he disliked always having to show his ignorance): 'Sounds like a visit to the tooth puller!'

'More pleasurable than that, I'd hope.'

'So what will they do for me, then?'

'Serve you, you dimwit!'

'Serve me how?'

'Well – you know! Or maybe you don't.' Felip gazed at him, thoughtfully. 'I guess you didn't have such things where you came from.'

'If we did, we didn't call them by that name.'

'Whores?' said Felip.

'Haws?' Hal repeated it, dubiously; the word meant nothing to him. He shook his head. 'Not that I know of.'

'No; I suppose you wouldn't have much use for them, really.' Felip laughed, almost disbelievingly. 'I reckon a visit's well overdue!'

He still didn't explain what the purpose of such a visit might be, but Hal thought perhaps it was wiser not to enquire too closely. It appeared that all the young men, at some time or another, were taken to the haws, which led him to believe it must be a kind of initiation rite – rather as the boys in the Boys' House had had one. It was part of the nature of initiation rites that you should be kept in ignorance until the moment arrived.

For the first time in a long time he thought of his year group, and in particular of his special friends, Andrew and Steven. He wondered if they ever thought of him – if they had missed him when he had gone away. They would be back in the community by now, fulfilling whatever roles they were deemed most suited for. Steven had been interested in medicine; he might have been encouraged to continue his studies. Andrew had been more practical, skilled in carpentry and good at growing things. Andrew would be easy to place.

'I'll tell you what!' Felip's bunched fist smote im amiably in the chest. 'No time like the present . . . we'll go down there tonight and get you sorted out!'

His first visit to the haws left him uncertain how he felt about it. The haws, he discovered, were exclusively women. They inhabited the narrow cobbled streets down by the harbour, living in dark, tumbledown cottages that let in the wind and the rain and the ever-pervading stench of fish.

'We'll get you one of the good 'uns,' said Felip. 'Always best, first time round. Some of the sour-faced bitches, you'd think they were doing you a favour.'

Afterwards, not knowing whether to feel triumphant at having been put to the test and proved himself a man, or degraded at having performed what he had always been taught to regard as an act of primitive bestiality, he couldn't escape the worrying notion that haw or not, his particular woman, good 'un that she was, had indeed been doing him a favour. He put the suggestion to Felip, who indignantly refuted it.

'There's no favour about it! That's what they're there for.'

'But do they enjoy it?' worried Hal.

'Never mind if *they* enjoy it! Did you, is more to the point?'

He said yes because he knew it was expected of him, though at that stage, if he were to be honest, he was still unsure.

'You don't want to worry about them.' Felip said it contemptuously. 'They're fed, they're clothed, they've got a roof over their heads . . . what more do they want?'

'I suppose they wouldn't do it if they didn't like it,' ventured Hal.

'They got no choice but to like it. It's that or nothing. They should think themselves lucky,' said Felip, 'that we find a use for 'em! We don't have to let 'em in.'

Hal could have asked, 'Let them in from where?'

but he chose not to. He told himself that he had displayed more than enough ignorance for one day.

Life settled into an agreeable routine. He went on fishing trips and learnt very quickly how to handle a boat: he paid regular visits, with Felip, to the haws down near the harbour: he amused himself in the intervals by flirting (he had learnt that that was the word) with Esta. Looking back on his own community, he failed now to see that it had had very much going for it. Tame, it seemed, in comparison with Cornishtown. If the men only knew what they were missing – and were not so greatly outnumbered by the women – there would be no more question of their allowing themselves to be civilised.

He had long since lost all qualms about whether the haws enjoyed what they were doing. They were there, and they did it, and that was all that mattered. After a drink or two one hardly cared. He had tried on a couple of occasions to talk to the one he generally used, a doe-eyed, pale-faced girl who might have been beautiful had she managed to smile now and again, but she had pinched her lips and made it very clear that she would rather he didn't.

'Talking is no part of our duties.'

She spoke with the accent of the Watchers. After that, he conducted his visits in silence.

By the time spring came round, he was receiving strong hints from Daniel that he ought to think of 'settling down' and marrying Esta. He was not totally convinced that he wanted to settle down: life as it was was too much fun. He discussed it with Felip, who pulled a face and said, 'It comes to us all, in the end. But it's not so bad . . . give 'em a string of brats to occupy 'em and they soon stop caring what you get up to. And you could do worse than marry Esta.'

He supposed that he could. Esta reminded him in some ways, with her constant teasing and the occasional challenges she threw out, of Elizabeth, though she had not Elizabeth's bold defiance and alert, questioning mind. Esta accepted the society she lived in – and, moreover, she attracted him physically, as poor little Elizabeth, crippled and ill-proportioned as she was, never could.

He decided he would pay one last visit to the haws – for, as soon as a man had agreed to marriage, the rules decreed that he behave himself, at least until the first child had been born. He would then go to Ansel and make an offer to take Esta off his hands.

His usual girl, with the doe eyes and pale face, had her front door shut, indicating that she was with someone else and not available. He walked on down the cobbled street, looking for a haw who could service him. He found an open door at a cottage he had never used before and stepped through into the tiny front room. The haw came forward to meet him.

It was Hanna.

Chapter Seven

The blush of horror and shame was on both their cheeks, but it was Hanna who broke the first appalled silence.

'Hal!' She came towards him, arms outstretched. 'My poor Hal! Try not to look so shocked.'

'I'm sorry,' he whispered. 'I'm sorry!'

'It's what happens to us. When we're sent away . . . did no one ever tell you?'

He shook his head, not trusting himself to speak. Hanna smiled; a brave, bright smile.

'This is the only use they can find for us. I suppose – ' her voice broke, but quickly recovered – 'I suppose we should count ourselves fortunate there's still some small service we can perform. In spite of our wickedness, we can still make some contribution to society.'

Anger came pulsing through him.

'What wickedness?' he shouted. 'When were you ever wicked?'

'I must have been, or the Power would not have punished me.'

'Hanna! You don't believe all that rubbish?'

'No – ' Her voice broke again: tears sprang to her eyes. 'No, but how else am I to make sense of it?'

'It's ignorance.' Hal said it bitterly. 'When you gave up learning, you lost all knowledge of the past.

You locked the door and you threw away the key! And what you substituted for it was claptrap!'

Hanna stood with bent head, as if under personal attack. Hal pursued the subject, brutally.

'It's taken the place of thought, hasn't it? Because it's easier than thinking. Anything you don't understand – put it down to the Power. Anything goes wrong – put it down to the Power. Don't bother looking for the real reasons. You know what the real reasons are? You know why all these kids are being born without arms and legs and their brains hanging outside their skulls?'

She winced.

'Do you want me to tell you? It's because you're ignorant! Because that thing you go and worship is slowly killing you, and the more faithful you are, and the more you worship, the more sick it's going to make you, the more kids you're going to have with three heads, and legs coming out of their belly-buttons, and if you'd taken the trouble to learn about the past you would have known that, just as I know, because it's there for anyone to read in old books and newspapers . . . that *thing*, that you call a shrine, was built by men to house power that was made by men – ' Hanna trembled slightly – 'and the only sensible thing to do is to keep as far away from it as you possibly can. Not gather round like a load of mindless idiots, staring at it till your eyeballs melt!'

'We've brought it on ourselves.' Hanna's voice was low, and trembled. 'Everything . . .' She covered her face with her hands. 'We've brought it all on ourselves!'

'But through ignorance,' urged Hal. 'Not wickedness. *You* never did anything wrong!'

'I went along with it.'

'What choice did you have?'

She took her hands from her face and looked at him, tearstained but calm.

'There's always a choice. I could have spoken out. I know that what you're saying is true. I think I've always known it. I think a lot of the women knew it. I could have said something.'

'But that would have been blasphemy!'

'The men would have called it so.'

'Yes, and what would they have done to you?'

'No more than they have already done. I'd have ended up here, as a server. But at least I would have spoken my mind! At least I might have given courage to others. I was too much of a coward. I hoped that if I kept my mouth shut, things would work out all right.'

'No one could blame you,' he muttered.

'I can blame me! I do blame me! If Elizabeth can speak out – ' She stopped. 'Hal,' she said, 'how are they all?'

He shuffled, uncomfortably.

'I don't know. I – I don't live with them any more.'

'I wondered. When you walked through the door . . . I thought you must have left. How long is it since – '

'This is my second summer coming up.' He said it gruffly, still embarrassed in her presence, sorry for having harangued her, ashamed of his own reason for coming.

'I always hoped, you know – ' she gave a little laugh, almost apologetic – 'that you might marry Elizabeth.'

'Elizabeth?' That took him by surprise; it was something that had never crossed his mind.

'She loved you so, and she's so vulnerable! I always thought that you were the one person who might be able to save her.'

He mumbled, 'Elizabeth wanted me to marry Anne. So did Mam and Amyas.'

'You didn't want to?'

'It wasn't that. I'd have had to become a Watcher.'

'Yes; and that's something you couldn't do. I can see that now. It never occurred to me before. I never realised how you felt. I always thought it was – something you'd just go along with.'

'I might have done if they hadn't made me go to the Shrine. When I saw what it was – I couldn't. Not even for Anne.'

'Could you for Elizabeth?'

He hesitated just a few seconds too long.

'I'm sorry,' she said. 'I shouldn't have asked that. It's only that I do worry about her so! No one will ever marry her – '

'Just because she's crippled?' He was indignant. The few members of his own community who had had the misfortune to be born less than physically perfect were treated with the same respect accorded everyone else.

'Partly because she's crippled. They treat it as a sin. They believe she's marked by the Power and that to marry her would bring disaster. But partly it's because she's been brave enough to speak her mind. Braver than I ever was. It's set people against her.'

'Yes.' He nodded, remembering what Judd and Pasco had said, all those years ago: come to a bad end, that one will. 'If it's any comfort,' he said, 'she doesn't do it so much any more. Ever since – you left. She's guarded her tongue.'

'That's almost worse!' cried Hanna. 'It means they've broken her spirit!'

'I don't think they've done that, exactly. I can't imagine anyone breaking Elizabeth's spirit. I think she still feels the same as she always did, she's just learned to be . . . a little cautious.'

'It still won't make anyone marry her.'

'Would that really matter?' Thinking of what happened to the Watchers' women once they were married, he couldn't help feeling that it might be a happy release.

'It would be terrible! You've no idea – ' Hanna choked – 'you've no idea how they would treat her! Her only hope would be if some horrid old man like Gideon Haggar agreed to take her.'

'Gideon Haggar?' He was revolted. 'He's seen more summers than Amyas!'

'Yes, and he's had almost as many wives! There are three of them down here – you don't get a second chance with him. Oh, Hal!' She gripped him with both hands. 'My poor Lizzie! What's to become of her? She'd never survive down here . . . she'd kill herself first! I told you, didn't I? There's always a choice, if you're brave enough to make one . . . Elizabeth's brave. And she's proud. She wouldn't allow herself to be used like this!'

'Hanna!' He pulled her closer, encircling her with his arms. 'There must be something we can do! There must be some way – '

'There isn't. Not for any of us.' She prised herself away from him. 'For me it's too late – and probably for Anne, as well. She'll be married by now. Maybe she'll be lucky. If not, she'll be joining the rest of us – and being Anne, she'll meekly accept that she's been wicked and that this is her punishment. Elizabeth won't ever accept it, she'll fight all the way and when she can't fight any more she'll kill herself. I begin to think it's what we should all have done!'

'What would happen if – if I were to marry you and we brought Elizabeth down here and looked after her?'

'Oh, Hal!' The tears glistened in Hanna's eyes. She touched him, very gently, on the cheek. 'That's the sweetest thought, and I love you for it, but you would never be allowed to marry me. You obviously don't know how the town people regard us. They see us as soiled goods – we *are* soiled goods! We're only allowed to exist so long as we serve their purpose. If they didn't have us, they would need to downgrade some of their own women, as they used to before we came. Now they have us, and it suits them very well. They don't intend to let any of us escape by getting married.'

'So if they won't let us get married, what's to stop us just setting up together?'

She smiled, sadly. 'You would then be a total

outcast. You would belong nowhere. They would regard you as their enemy.'

He could see that what she was saying was probably correct.

'I could still bring Elizabeth down and marry her.'

'Oh, Hal, if only you could!'

'Why couldn't I?'

'They would never allow her in. If you said she'd been rejected they'd take her as a server. If you said she hadn't been rejected, they'd send her straight back. They don't want trouble. They'd rather have us as their friends than as their enemies. We're more use to them that way.'

'So you're saying there's nothing we can do?' He refused to accept it. 'There has to be something!'

'There is one thing.' Hanna said it slowly. 'But it's the only thing I can think of.'

'What? Tell me and I'll do it!'

'Don't be too eager, you might not want to.'

'Try me!'

'If you took Elizabeth and left.'

'Left? You mean – '

'Back to your own community.'

He was stunned. A thousand objections instantly rushed to his mind.

'But – how could I? I don't know the way!'

'I'm sure you could find it.'

Of course he could find it. If Daniel had found it, Hal could.

'What is the problem?' She looked at him, gravely. 'Would they not accept her?'

'They'd accept her,' he muttered. 'I'm the one they wouldn't accept.'

'You? But – oh! I was forgetting.' Her face reddened. 'You do things to your men that you would not want done.'

He said awkwardly. 'I'm sure you might think it was best they should be done.'

'It's not for me to say. I ought not to have suggested it. I had no right.'

'You had every right,' he protested; but feebly enough.

There was a pause.

'I'm neglecting my duties,' said Hanna. 'I'm not kept fed and sheltered just to talk to people. You came here for a quite other purpose.' She crossed the room and held open a door. 'Please come through,' she said.

It was his turn to redden. He did so, deeply and painfully.

'Now you're trying to punish me!'

'No! I'm not! But since there's nothing to be done you might as well use me as you obviously wish to use me and let me get on with my life – such as it is.'

'If you really think,' said Hal, 'that I could go ahead and – do that to you – '

'Why not?' She faced him, defiantly. 'How am I any different from any of the other women you've used? Simply because you know me! Do you think they don't suffer as I do? Do you think they don't feel every bit as polluted and degraded? I wish,' she cried, 'that I had the courage to end it all!'

'Hanna,' he begged, 'please!'

'Leave me.' She whirled past him, to the front door. 'Go and make use of someone else and close your eyes to their suffering! I don't ever want to see you again!'

He did not make use of anyone else, neither did he go to Ansel and make his offer for Esta. He lay awake through the night, conducting arguments with his conscience. He had not asked to be brought into this community and abandoned amongst them. He was fond of Elizabeth but saw no reason that he should be expected to ruin his life for her. There was no way, having tasted the fruits of manhood, that he was going to go back and surrender them. And, in any case, there was no guarantee that Elizabeth would wish to go back with him to his own community. She had once declared that she would like to, but that had been in the old days, before she became a reformed character. Elizabeth was just as much a product of her society as anyone else. Probably by now she was every bit as conformist as Anne. And even if she weren't, how was he supposed to smuggle her away from her family without being detected? The whole thing was a complete nonsense.

The following morning he left on an extended fishing trip with Ansel and Felip and did his best to forget all about it.

Of course, he couldn't. Hanna's face haunted him, her words reproached him. Felip rubbed his hands gleefully as they put into harbour.

'You and me? Tonight? Down Haws' Alley?'

The blood rushed to his cheeks.

'I've – decided. I'm not going there any more.'

'Hey, hey! What's all this? Do I smell marriage in the air?' Felip tipped back his head and flared his nostrils. 'It seems that I do! Hal's going to be a good boy from now on, everybody!'

Hal smiled, weakly. He endured the ribbing as best he could, and only hoped that news of it would not reach Esta. He was in no way bound to Esta, but for all that would not like to raise false expectations. He had been prepared to make an offer for her – but that had been before he discovered Hanna. Before he had been forced, at last, to face an unpalatable truth which he had been avoiding for far too long. The thought of any woman being condemned to a life of servitude was appalling enough: the thought of it happening to Elizabeth was quite simply intolerable.

As soon as he could, he slipped away and started up the hillside. The guards were on the gate, but it was not difficult to evade them. There were ways round if you were familiar with the terrain, and besides, for lack of stimulus they were none too vigilant. The last strangers to have appeared were David and Keren, with Hal. It was difficult to be constantly on the alert when nothing ever happened.

He approached the Watchers' cluster of dwellings more warily than he had skirted the guards. Unlike the men of Cornishtown, the Watchers had no use for guns – not because they disapproved of killing but because guns were artefacts from the past. They were not averse, however, to the knotted rope or the length of birch, and Hal had no desire to be sent back down the hill with his back in ribbons and the flesh hanging off him in strips.

He secreted himself at the edge of the woods and settled down for what he knew could be a long wait. He saw Mam quite quickly, but she was with one of the other women and it was a risk he daren't take. There was then a long interval before he saw another member of the family: Anne. He needed to think fast. He had hoped for Elizabeth, but on the other hand Anne was on her own. Could she be trusted?

'Anne!' He hissed it out of the side of his mouth.

She sprang round, startled. Too late, he saw that she was pregnant. He cursed his luck: he would never have attracted her attention had he known. Pregnancy was one long terror to the Watcher women; at such times, anything which smacked even remotely of blasphemy was shunned.

It would be undisputed blasphemy to acknowledge him. It would probably even be blasphemy to go on her way and ignore him. Duty would demand that she alert the men a heretic was in their midst.

He braced himself for flight, while he waited to see what she would do. He saw her stop, and peer uncertainly into the woods. Her face, as she caught sight of him, grew apprehensive. Would she turn and run? He tensed, ready to do likewise, but then, glancing nervously about her, she moved quickly towards him.

'Why are you here? Don't you know it's dangerous?'

'I have to talk to you. Come!'

He seized her hand and dragged her deeper into

the shelter of the trees. She went with him, unprotesting. He reflected that if anyone should stumble upon them she could always, with some truth, claim that he had abducted her.

'I've seen Hanna,' said Hal. 'I've spoken with her.'

Her face became an expressionless mask. Her voice devoid of all emotion, she said: 'I know no one called Hanna.'

'Then if you know no one called Hanna you should know no one called Hal! I'm the one who blasphemed, not her! She never did anything wrong, and you know it!'

There was a pause. Anne looked down to her feet and remained stubbornly silent. He reflected that this way he would get nothing out of her. Like all the women – excepting only Elizabeth – she was terrified. Even just coming into the woods with him was an act of bravery.

More gently, he said: 'When is the baby due?'

'Very soon, I think.'

He had forgotten their aversion to measuring time.

'Will you be fit to make the pilgrimage?' By his calculation, the annual trip should be taking place any day now, for he realised that their aim was to arrive for midsummer.

'Oh, yes,' she said. And then, tonelessly: 'We are going to stay up there.'

'You and – your husband?'

'Luke and I, and all of us. Mam, Da, Elizabeth . . . I think that it will kill Elizabeth.'

He didn't try telling her that in the long run it

would probably kill all of them. It would be a waste of breath and could very well scare her off before he had achieved the purpose of his visit.

'Anne!' He stretched out a hand: she backed away from him in something like panic. 'Anne, will you do something for me? Will you tell Elizabeth that I'm here?'

She looked at him, dubiously.

'Tell her I'll be in our old meeting place; she'll know what it means. Please, Anne! For Elizabeth's sake. I can't do anything for you or Hanna, but I might just possibly be able to save her.'

He could see the struggle taking place in her mind.

'You just said – ' he reminded her of it, sharply – 'that going back would kill her.'

'She would kill herself. That is what she told me.'

'Then knowing Elizabeth, that is exactly what she would do.'

'It would be blasphemy,' muttered Anne.

'Do you think she would care a fig for that?'

'That is her whole problem! She has never cared a fig! All these things that are happening – '

He felt the anger rising in him.

'Don't you try to blame Elizabeth,' he said. 'She's not responsible.'

'She has hardly helped herself.'

'What could she have done? Was it her fault she was born with a crippled foot and an inquiring mind?'

'She would do better to have accepted, like the rest of us.'

'So you will be quite happy to let her kill herself?

You would rather that than make shift to help me save her?'

Anne raised troubled eyes to his.

'Can you really save her?'

'I should hope to do so, but I need your help. I need to speak to her.'

'And then?'

'I should take her away with me.'

'They would come after you.'

'Not if I arranged it so that it looked as though she had done what she was threatening to do.'

The colour drained from Anne's cheeks.

'You would make it seem as though she had killed herself?'

'It would be necessary,' he said. 'But at least you would know the truth. And you could tell Mam.' He wouldn't want Mam thinking that Elizabeth was dead.

In a low voice, Anne said: 'To take one's life is blasphemy.'

'But she wouldn't have taken her life! That's the very thing we're trying to avoid. She would be safe with me.'

'To go with a blasphemer is also blasphemy . . . to go with a blasphemer is the biggest blasphemy of all.'

That was it, then. He was lost – and so was Elizabeth.

'But I think,' said Anne, 'that it would finish Mam if anything were to happen to Lizzie.'

He clutched, desperately, at the straw she was offering. 'Mam has surely had enough sorrow in her life.'

'It has been nothing but sorrow.'

'So will you not help me save her from yet more?'

A shuddering sigh shook Anne's body. Closing her eyes, she made a sign across her breast. He had seen the Watcher women do this before. He had asked Elizabeth, once, what it signified, and she had giggled – for she had still been young enough, then, to giggle and be happy – and had told him, 'It's supposed to ward off evil spirits.'

Anne opened her eyes. 'I've already sinned,' she said, 'so I shall be punished anyway. Wait here, or wherever it is you are going to wait. I'll send her to you.'

He retreated to the den in the heart of the woods, where all those years ago he had taught Elizabeth her letters. He hadn't long to wait. She came running to him, undeterred by her crippled foot or the brambles which tore at her.

'Hal!'

'Hush!' He placed a finger to his lips.

'What are you doing here? If they caught you, they'd string you up!'

'As bad as that?' He had anticipated a beating at the worst. 'In that case, they must not catch me – nor you, either.'

'Oh! Me!' She pulled a face. 'They can do what they like with me. I no longer care what they do with me. They say they're going to make me go back with them, but they're not! They can't force me.'

'I fear they could,' he said.

'Well, they couldn't, for I should kill myself first!'

'Let us have no more talk of killing.' He took

her hands, holding them tightly. 'Did Anne not tell you why I came?'

She shook her head. 'She only said where to find you.'

'Which you did very speedily! I was hoping you might. Now, listen! Do you remember, a long time ago, you said you'd like to come back with me to my community?'

'Yes – ' She was looking up at him with a kind of eager trustfulness, yet the tone of her voice was carefully neutral.

'Would you still like to come back with me?'

'Oh, Hal – ' She whispered the words almost fearfully, as if even now he might only be teasing her.

'Can you meet me here after dark? Is that possible?'

'Yes!'

'You're quite sure?'

'Yes, yes!'

'Because if there's any doubt you'd better start hiding out straight away.'

'I'll be here!'

'Very well, but don't try bringing anything with you, we shall have to travel light. And whatever you do, don't say a word to a single soul, not even Anne. All right?'

'Right!'

He bent, and kissed her.

'Don't let me down! I'm relying on you.'

Back in town, Hal made his way down to the harbour, to the web of narrow streets and huddled cottages. Hanna's door was standing ajar. He tapped on it.

Hanna blushed scarlet when she saw who it was.

'Since when did anyone extend the courtesy of knocking at a servant's door? I'm surprised you don't just march in.'

'Hanna, shut up!' he said. 'It's not what you think. I'm taking Elizabeth away, but we can't leave immediately, I need to arrange things. Can you hide her here with you for a day or so?'

'I – yes! Of course! But – '

'You're sure she'll be safe?'

'Safer here than anywhere so long as she stays within doors, b– '

'She'll do whatever I tell her to do. I'm picking her up as soon as it's dark, I'll bring her straight away. Can you arrange to keep your door closed?'

'I'll see to it. Oh, Hal! I can't thank you enough! But – '

He cut her short. 'Please don't thank me. I feel too guilty for that.'

'You? Guilty? Why?'

'The way I've . . . used the others. Without even thinking about it. The fact that I have to leave you here.'

'Don't worry about that! It's enough that you're saving Elizabeth. No one could ask more of you. But, Hal! If you go back – ' She looked at him, searchingly. 'Won't they – do things to you?'

'I imagine they will,' he said. 'I'm trying my best not to think about it.'

He spent the next few days squirrelling away food

supplies for the journey – biscuits, cheese, fresh fruit and vegetables: nuts, dried fruit, a loaf of bread. He had no idea of how to reach Croydon travelling overland so had decided they would have to go by boat, taking the same route as Daniel had taken and trusting to luck that London was still negotiable.

Securing a boat presented no problems, but he was concerned that as soon as they discovered its loss, and the fact that he was gone, they would send one of the larger and faster fishing vessels in pursuit. They would not know that he had Elizabeth with him, for Elizabeth to all intents and purposes was dead: she had drowned herself in the sea, leaving her clothes behind her on the beach to bear witness. But they would be angry enough with Hal to go after him. There seemed to him only one solution: he would have to wait till the entire fleet set sail, find some way of not going with them, then steal out in the early hours of the morning. It would give him ample time to slip round the coast and be well on his way before the boats returned.

It was simple enough to fake a stomach upset, though he felt sorry for Dorothy, fussing over him as he rolled and writhed in his bed, shouting out in occasional bouts of agony. He kept it up for several hours after the fleet had sailed, until in the end he had exhausted himself and quite naturally fell asleep.

He stole from the house before Dorothy was up. He took with him a fishing rod, the *A-Z* from Daniel's cupboard, a firearm and a further generous helping of provisions from the larder. His conscience slightly troubled him, for Dorothy had done him no wrong, but Daniel would have kept him here against his will: he had no conscience where Daniel was concerned.

He had thought at first he would be forced to hole all the remaining vessels, mainly small dinghies and coracles, in order to prevent the man coming after him, but in the event Daniel had taken Hal's place in Ansel's boat so he was spared that particular vandalistic task.

He and Elizabeth slipped away with the first light of morning. Hanna had crept down to the beach to see them off. Her last whispered words to Hal were, 'Take care of her for me! And I trust your people spare you.'

Reflecting on what he had seen, both in Cornishtown and amongst the Watchers, he could think of no very good reason that they should.

Chapter Eight

In deciding to make the journey by sea, Hal had forgotten the Watchers' prohibition against going on water. He was forcibly reminded of it by Elizabeth's violent trembling as the boat cast off.

'You're surely not scared?' he said, bracingly. 'Not with me?'

Her teeth chattered and she clung, white-knuckled, with both hands to the edge of her seat.

'Oh, now, come!' he said, trying to jolly her along. The last thing he wanted was Elizabeth falling apart. 'You know all that business about the Power was nonsense! You've always known it. Otherwise why would you have uttered all those terrible blasphemies? Shall I tell you what Judd and Pasco used to say? That Elizabeth, they used to say, she'll come to a bad end!'

Elizabeth tried to smile, but it was a woebegone attempt.

'Look at me,' said Hal. 'I've been on the water dozens of times – scores of times. That many times!' He held out ten fingers, and again, and again. 'Nothing's happened to me, has it?' Dutifully, she shook her head. 'So nothing will happen to you. Take my word for it.'

There was a silence, and he thought that he had settled her fears; but then, 'I heard – ' she said.

'What did you hear?'

'I heard – one of Hanna's friends. She said – '

He waited.

'She was talking about – someone – called Felip. She said . . . I hope next time he goes to sea he doesn't come back.'

'I suppose he must have upset her.' He wondered if Felip had been more than ordinarily cavalier, or if the haws routinely wished the men of Cornishtown to drown at sea. He could hardly blame them if they did.

'What did she mean?' Elizabeth lifted a small and anxious face to his. 'How should he not come back?'

'Oh, well! Taking an extreme case . . . if the weather were bad, say. Say there was a storm at sea – '

'What? What would happen?'

'Nothing that is in the least likely to happen to us. A man might fall overboard or the vessel might founder. But not,' Hal said firmly, 'in this kind of weather. Only when the sea is rough and the boats are going far out in search of fish. Not the way we are travelling, close in to the shore.'

He stayed as close in as he dared, but he knew from the tales Daniel had told that there were stretches of coast where it was unwise to take a boat into shallow waters. It was fortunate that in all innocence, purely out of interest, he had encouraged Daniel during the dark nights of last winter to talk of his exploits. They had even pored together over an old map, with Daniel pointing out to him the various danger zones.

He could see the map, now, could see the bays and inlets, recall some of the names that had been printed there . . . Portland Bill, the Isle of Wight,

Beachy Head . . . he could see Daniel's finger stabbing down on to the map.

'That bit there . . . that's best avoided. Nearly come to grief there, I did.'

Hal charted their course with the image of the map ever present in his mind. Elizabeth bore up well until the first of the large waves hit them. There was no danger of their capsizing, he was too experienced a sailor by now to allow that to happen, but he had his hands full enough at the tiller without the added burden of having to stop and comfort her.

'It's all right!' He made his voice as reassuring as possible. 'Nothing's going to happen.'

She went on cowering in the bottom of the boat, hands held protectively over her head. He had no time to soothe her out of it, his priority must be to keep them afloat. Another wave came, slapping against them and lifting them momentarily out of the water. It was then that she started screaming, and invoking the name of the Power.

'Great-Power-that-art-in-everything-have-mercy! Forgive-me-my-sins-and-all-evil-thoughts!'

It shook him, hearing such imbecilic babble coming from Elizabeth, of all people. He had not realized the grip that her upbringing had had on her. In moments of stress, it seemed, she threw common sense to the winds and reverted to the state of mindless credulity in which she had been reared.

He knew that she could not be held to blame; all the same, it irritated him, at a time when he could have done with some support. Here he was, risking life and limb, and ultimately even his very manhood, in order to rescue her from the same life of degradation to which her sister had been condemned, and all she could think to offer by way of return was a fit of screaming hysterics whilst he battled single-handed to maintain them on an even keel.

'Great-Power-save-me! Have-mercy! Forgive-me-m- '

'*Elizabeth!*' In his fury and confusion, he leaned forward and he fetched her a blow across the face which sent her rocketing backwards. He was instantly remorseful, but it had the desired effect: the screaming stopped.

As soon as he could he lashed the tiller and went to her, crouching by her side, coaxing her off her knees and into his arms.

'Elizabeth, I'm sorry! I'm sorry!' Agonised, he rocked her to and fro, as he had seen women rock their babies. He had never thought that he would use violence. 'Forgive me! I didn't mean to hurt you.'

'You didn't hurt me.' She was calm, now. 'You did what had to be done.'

He was forgetting that of course she was accustomed to be hit. Ruefully, he said, 'I panicked. I couldn't think of any other way to stop you. But you see, I – I need your help. We're not in any danger, the boat isn't going to sink, you're not going to drown, but if we're going to get anywhere we have to work as a team . . . I need to be able to rely on you.'

'Tell me what I must do,' she said. 'I won't be silly again, I promise.'

He could see that she was ashamed, and that made two of them. From that point on they worked together, and if she still trembled when the swell heaved beneath them at least there were no more hysterics.

'You should have brought Hanna,' she said one day, with a sigh.

He had thought of doing so, but truth to tell he had been scared of the vengeance that might have been wreaked on his own people had he made off with what the men of Cornishtown considered their property.

'We should have needed a larger boat,' he said, lamely.

'I didn't mean that! I meant you should have brought Hanna instead of me. She would have been of more help to you.'

'You're doing splendidly,' he said.

'But I was silly. Hanna wouldn't have been. Hanna's brave.'

'Hanna *is* brave,' he agreed, 'but not more so than you. I can't help remembering that you spoke out when others kept quiet.'

'Yes, and what good did it do?' she cried. 'It might have been better had I held my tongue. I only caused trouble for everyone.'

'You voiced the thoughts that the other women had. At least thanks to you they knew they were not alone.'

'They knew that anyway,' she muttered. 'They used to talk when the men weren't there.'

'The difference is that you used to talk when the men were there. You were the only one who had the courage to do so. If others had joined you – '

'They couldn't.' She shook her head. 'They had too much to lose. It was different for me . . . I always knew that I had no future.'

He squeezed her hand. 'You have now.'

Doubtfully, she said: 'Will your people really accept me?'

'Accept you? They'll do more than just accept you, they'll welcome you with open arms.'

'And you?' she said.

He wasn't so sure about that.

It was Elizabeth who saw the smoke, a thin plume of it curling up from somewhere inland. Hal was uncertain which part of the coast they were at. They had sailed round the large mass of land which he thought must be the Isle of Wight, and past a promontory which might or might not have been Beachy Head. They were as yet, by his estimation, nowhere near the headland which was one of the spots Daniel had marked as hazardous, and round which they had to sail to reach the estuary of the Thames, to take them through to London. It looked possible to put in to land, should they decide to do so.

They hove to and discussed it, watching all the time as the plume of smoke danced and hovered, tantalisingly close. Where there was smoke there had presumably to be fire; but fire, as Hal pointed out, did not necessarily mean people. Elizabeth, on the other hand, argued that it most probably did, and that people spelt danger. Yet why should they? thought Hal. His own community had not harmed Daniel, Daniel's community had not harmed him. Even the Watchers had been prepared to accept him so long as he had not presumed to question.

'What shall we do? Shall we take a look, or not?'

Elizabeth was all for pushing on; Hal was the one who hesitated. He kept remembering the question he had put to David and Keren all those years ago, when they had made the journey to Cornishtown.

'If there are other people out there, why haven't we gone in search of them?'

And Keren's withering reply: 'Because we're too scared. We don't know what we might find, and we don't think we want to know, thank you very much!'

He couldn't help reflecting what a feather in his cap it would be were he to turn up not only with Elizabeth but with news of another community. They might then see that the uncivilised male did have some redeeming features, for what was the other thing Keren had said?

'We need you . . . men, as nature made them. Our muscles have grown flabby for want of use.'

'I think we should just put in,' said Hal, 'and have a quick look.' It was too good an opportunity to miss. 'You can stay with the boat, if you like, while I jump out and scout around.'

'No!' She clutched at him. 'If you're going, I'm coming with you!'

'You mean you're more scared that you might have to put to sea by yourself than of falling into the hands of cannibals?' he teased; but she didn't know what cannibals were and it seemed, on the whole, best not to go into explanations.

They ran the boat up onto the shingle and set off across the stony and deserted beach in the direction of the plume of smoke, now wavering thinly over the top of a high ridge of sand dune. Taking no chances, Hal had brought his gun with him. He had not yet learnt to fear people the way Elizabeth did, but he knew rather better than he had in the old days why Daniel had not set forth unarmed. It might strike his own community as barbarous, but it seemed to Hal no more than good sense.

Gesturing to Elizabeth to stay where she was, he crept forward, on hands and knees, up to the crest of the sand dune. Cautiously, he raised his head. The sight that he saw both repelled and unnerved him. Round a smouldering fire were squatted a group of perhaps twenty to thirty human beings – but such human beings as he had never in his life seen before. Dwarfish, twisted, misshappen, they hunkered about the burning embers. They appeared to be a mix of males and females, though at a first glance, so distorted were their forms, it was impossible to be sure. Such limbs as they had – such limbs as grew where nature intended limbs to grow – were covered in the rags and remnants of twentieth-century garb such as his own community still wore.

Sickened, feeling that he had seen enough, Hal was about to slither back down the sand dune when a sudden distressed cry from Elizabeth made him turn. Two malformed shapes were approaching her at a kind of crouching run.

'Stop that!'

Hal plunged back, floundering and sinking in the soft sand, only to be speedily overtaken by the more fleet-footed of the fire-squatters, alerted like him by Elizabeth's cry but unencumbered by shoes and moving faster than he.

As they hopped and skipped their way past him they uttered small shrill cries, like the chirruping of birds. Reaching Elizabeth, they twittered and chirped in a state of excitement, dabbing at her and palping with hands which in some cases grew directly from hunched shoulders and in others ended not in fingers but in strange ungainly clumps.

'Leave her!' yelled Hal.

A breakaway band were now encircling him. A small pink creature, completely bald with eyes that had slipped halfway down its face, stretched out to grab at him. Another, with slits where its nose should have been, contorted a lipless mouth into the parody of a smile.

Hal recoiled instinctively, backing into the path of some stragglers, including one with no eyes being led by another which he at first thought had two heads but which, he realised belatedly, was two bodies fused together.

The noseless one came at him, waving hands like fronds, the lipless mouth munching on air in some kind of silent ecstasy.

'Back!' Hal raised his gun, intending to fire it, if at all, over their heads, but the lipless one, emitting a series of eager squeaks, flung himself forward, fronds reaching out to take possession.

'Back!' screamed Hal.

He swore to himself afterwards that the gun went off without his meaning it to; it may well have been so. In his panic and revulsion, he had scarcely known what he was doing. Either way, the result was the same.

As the shot rang out, the distorted bodies whirled and scattered in a chaos of terror and confusion. One by one they fled the scene, until only the man with no eyes was left, piteously whimpering as he groped his way after his companions. The lipless one lay where he had fallen.

Hal raced forward and seized Elizabeth by the hand.

'Quick! Before they come back!'

'But what about – '

'It's dead. There's nothing we can do for it. Run!'

It wasn't until they were on their way, at sea again, that the nausea came upon him. He turned his head and retched, painfully and emptily, over the side of the boat.

'Hal?' Elizabeth touched him timidly on the shoulder. 'Are you sick?'

'Only with myself.'

'It wasn't your fault! You couldn't help it.'

'They were unarmed.'

'But there were so many of them!'

'And who's to say they would have harmed us?'

'You didn't know – you couldn't take the chance!'

He refused to be solaced. He thought that he would hear the cries of the lipless man to his own dying day.

That night, despite Elizabeth's protests, he threw the gun overboard.

The following morning, the dawn light revealed a bleak and desolate coastline, bare of all vegetation, stretching further into the distance than the eye could follow.

'Look!' Elizabeth pointed. 'Do you think that's another shrine?'

Hal switched his gaze and saw a cluster of great grey blocks, and beyond them what looked like an army of metal giants striding across the empty marshland.

'I don't know,' he said, 'but whatever it is we shall keep well away from it.'

He had always known that the worst part of the journey was yet to come. David had told him years ago that the big cities were best avoided; Daniel himself had admitted that crossing London had been an unnerving experience. For all that, he thought it best not to alert Elizabeth but simply to take it as it came. They had no alternative but to get through London somehow, for he knew of no other route.

The journey proved every bit as hair-raising as Daniel had promised. From the moment they tied the boat up at the spot marked by Daniel on the *A-Z* – the bridges, fortunately, still stood, or they would have been in even more serious trouble – it was a question of slowly picking their way round and over vast mounds of fallen masonry. Elizabeth, with her crippled foot, struggled valiantly but found the going next to impossible. She made no complaints but he could tell that she was failing, and in the end, ignoring her protests, he hoisted her onto his back and carried her.

Rats, even as Daniel had described, were everywhere, running quite boldly and openly all about them; and even now, a hundred and fifty years after the plague had cleared the streets of teeming humanity, the buildings which that humanity had erected, buildings such as Hal had never dreamt of, towering monumentally into the sky, were slowly crumbling, collapsing, throwing off great chunks of themselves into what remained of the streets.

Yet it was neither his burden nor the rats nor the disintegrating buildings which caused Hal the most concern. Most of the streets marked by Daniel had been major ones – not motorways, but 'A' roads, according to the reference section at the front of the *A-Z*. They were still just about discernible. Scrub might encroach and ivy crawl ever upwards, trees and brambles might fill the gaps left over the decades where buildings had sickened and finally died, but the roads had been wide and traces remained provided they looked diligently enough and sought enough clues.

The worry was not so much that they would irrevocably lose themselves as that their supply of fresh water would run out. Given time and care Hal felt reasonably confident that he could ultimately lead them to their destination, but progress was of necessity slow. He had, perhaps foolishly, not reckoned on having to carry Elizabeth.

'If it weren't for me,' she sobbed, at one point, 'you might have been there by now!'

And then she reflected, and sobbed even harder.

'If it weren't for me, you wouldn't have to be making this journey at all!'

'It was my own choice,' he said.

'I don't believe it was, I believe Hanna pushed you into it!'

'She put the idea into my head; that is all.'

'She had no right!'

'She had every right – just as I had every right to say no, if that was how I felt.'

'She made you feel bad about things.'

He stiffened. 'What things?'

'Not becoming one of us. Not marrying Anne.'

'That had nothing whatsoever to do with it!' He was happy to be able to assure her of it. 'I did what I did because I couldn't bear the thought of you being carted off to live with those maniacs. I did it entirely of my own free will. No one pushed me, browbeat me, or made me feel guilty.' She was silent. 'Well?' he said. 'Do you hear me complaining?'

Elizabeth sighed. 'I suppose not. But it's true that if it weren't for me you wouldn't have to be doing it!'

They came at last to the road which led to Croydon, and the going became less hazardous. The buildings here had not perhaps been as imposing as the buildings in the capital, for the piles of rubble were generally smaller and easier to skirt round. Elizabeth was able to walk, Hal to relax.

'In the early years,' he said, for he knew the history of his own community, 'they used to come scavenging here.'

He could see that the concept meant nothing to her.

'Removing everything they thought would be useful,' he explained, 'before the buildings started to collapse.'

'What sort of things?'

'Anything! Clothes, food, tools – medicines, books. We have hundreds of books you'll be able to read.'

'That will be nice,' she said, soberly.

'Well, come on!' A bit of enthusiasm might have been in order. 'I thought that's what you always wanted?'

'It was – it is!'

'So you might try to sound just a little bit happy! What's the matter?'

She spoke without looking at him. 'Wasn't there a girl in Cornishtown you were going to marry?'

'So what if there was?'

'How can I be happy,' she burst out, 'knowing that?'

He was silent, trying to sort out the implications.

'Who told you?' he said, at last.

'I heard Hanna discussing it with one of the others.'

She spoke of Hanna quite often, with regret but without any apparent sign of distress. He concluded that she had no idea of the life that her sister was forced to lead. He himself would certainly not enlighten her.

'A girl called Esta, they said. They said – ' her top lip quivered – 'they said you were making a big sacrifice.'

'There was a girl called Esta, and maybe I might have married her, but it was not such a big sacrifice as all that.'

Looking back, he realised he had never felt any strong attachment to Esta. She had simply been the first girl to rouse those strong physical emotions to which Linden and her ilk took such violent exception. He fancied that her feelings for him had not run very much deeper. He had been something a little different, a little out of the ordinary, and it had amused her to flirt with him. Already she would be off and away after someone else.

'You must have loved her,' objected Elizabeth.

He took her hand to help her round a fallen parapet.

'Had I loved her, don't you think I would have brought her with me?'

She digested this. It seemed for a while to content her, but then suddenly and with obvious dismay she cried, 'You won't ever be able to get married now! Not if they do things to you!'

'So I won't,' he said, gravely.

She obviously felt that he was mocking her.

'Don't laugh, it's not funny! And it's all m-my fault!'

Elizabeth stumbled and would have fallen had he not had her hand grasped very firmly in his. Already the tears were starting to her eyes. 'I should have thought about it! I should have refused to come! Oh, Hal – ' She sank to her knees, her head drooping forward. 'Why don't you just leave me here and go back?'

'Now, look,' he said. He squatted by her side,

ineffectually blotting at her eyes with the edge of his shirt. 'I haven't come all this way to have you collapse on me. Be brave! We're nearly there.'

'But what will they do to you?' wept Elizabeth.

'Who? My people? Nothing I can't cope with,' he said, though truth to tell it gave him nightmares just thinking about it, which was why, for the most part, he kept it locked away in a remote corner of his brain where he could not easily get at it. Too much morbid dwelling on his likely fate and he doubted he would ever have embarked on the journey. 'Who knows?' he said, cheerfully. 'Maybe they won't do anything to me . . . maybe they'll make an honorary exception.'

Elizabeth turned a tearstained face towards him. 'Do you really think so?'

No, he didn't really think so, not if Linden were still around; but he had never known Elizabeth anything but proud and defiant. It upset him to see her humbled, weeping with guilt and fatigue and a sense of helplessness.

Ignoring the pains in his own aching shoulders and blistered feet, he swung her up into his arms.

'Just don't worry about it,' he said.

Chapter Nine

For the first few days after his return, limping back with Elizabeth in his arms, Hal found himself a hero. Everyone wanted to hear the story of how he and Elizabeth had sailed round the coast and up the Thames to London. The entire community gathered to listen as they told of their adventures. By some mutual but unspoken consent, for they had never discussed it between them, neither Hal nor Elizabeth mentioned the incident of the plume of smoke and the small band of misshapen people that had crouched by the fire. Later, perhaps, Hal would make his confession, for his own behaviour still weighed heavily on his conscience; but for now he had enough to cope with, finding his feet as he strove to come to terms with yet another new way of life.

Initially, staggering with exhaustion and on the brink of collapse, he had been past caring about anything save the need to sink down and rest. It wasn't until he had slept his fill that they broke the news to him, David and Keren between them: April had died six months ago.

'If only you had come when we sent for you!' There had been more of sorrow in David's voice than reproach.

With Keren, it had been just the opposite:

'She wanted so much to see you before she went.'

He had protested vigorously, feeling himself under attack.

'I never knew that you had sent for me! Are you saying that you finally won the vote?'

'Almost two years ago.'

The implications for his future had not immediately sunk in; there had been too much else to wrestle with. Not only the fact of April's death, but Daniel's apparent duplicity. Two years ago Hal had still been with the Watchers: it would have been easy enough for Daniel to keep him in ignorance.

'You actually sent people? They actually got through?'

'Andrew and Steven; yes.' Keren had furrowed her brow; wondering, no doubt, whether he was to be trusted. 'We chose them specially, because they were your friends. They told us that their message had been passed to you and the answer had come back that you were quite settled where you were and had no wish to return.'

'The message never reached me!'

'Did it not?' David had gazed at him, sadly. 'I wish April might have known. It hurt her so much.'

'For your information – ' Hal had felt a flash of angry self-pity – 'for your information, they never had the least intention of letting me come back. Never! Right from the very beginning!'

At this, there had been a puzzled silence.

'But why ever not?' had said Keren, at last.

Such simpletons these people were! Such simpletons!

'They like to keep hold of all the men they can get.'

'For procreation?'

'No!' He had spat it at them, contemptuously. 'For defence!'

The puzzlement had, if anything, increased.

'Defence against what?'

'Attack!' What else?

Keren, very gravely, had said, 'But who should attack them?'

'Anyone – anything! For all they know, there could be nine million savage tribes out there just waiting to pounce. They have to be prepared.'

Slowly, and disbelievingly, Keren had shaken her head. David had continued looking at him a while longer, as if struggling to make sense of what he had just heard. In the end he had abandoned the attempt and said simply, 'So they never gave you the message.'

'That's right!' He had got it at last. 'They never gave me the message.'

'I wish that April could have known.'

Well, she didn't, thought Hal. And whose fault was that? He had never asked to be sent away.

'You'd have thought,' he said, 'that it might have occurred to one of those crap arses – ' he had deliberately used the most vulgar expression he could think of: he had had an obscure desire to shock, or even wound – 'it might have occurred to them to wonder why I never came and spoke to them? Why I never explained in person?'

'Perhaps it should have done.' Keren, reluctantly, had acknowledged the point. 'At the time they simply accepted what they were told.'

'Keep their brains in their backsides,' had sneered Hal.

He later came to realise that in all probability they had been only too happy to be duped, and to go back without him; but in those first few days after his return such an idea would not have entered his head. People were indignant when they heard how he had been tricked, full of praise for the way he had escaped and approval at having brought Elizabeth with him.

Elizabeth, in fact, was his trump card, for despite the vote having at last been carried there were still those, mainly of the older generation, including the ever-implacable Linden, who could only view an uncivilised male with repugnance and extreme mistrust. His treatment of Elizabeth, and her obvious fondness for him, contributed at least a few points in his favour.

It was some time, however, before it dawned on him that even amongst his contemporaries he was not universally held to be a hero, nor unreservedly welcomed back into the community. He began noticing that whenever he tried to move in on a group of youths his own age there was an air of unease, almost of hostility. In the end he could stand it no longer but tackled Steven outright.

'Why do you all behave as if you resent me?'

'How would you expect us to behave? You think we should throw our arms around you and embrace you?'

'We used to be friends,' protested Hal.

'We used to be. Once.'

'Can't we still?'

'On what basis –' Steven curled his lip – 'can you and I be friends? Now?'

'You mean because I was sent away and you weren't? Does it really make such a difference?'

'You tell me,' suggested Steven.

It did make a difference; of course it did. He could not deny it. But who then was he to be friends with?

'Are you saying you're all going to shun me?'

'Not as a conscious act. But put yourself in our position . . . how would you feel? You're part of the new order; you're all right. We're the ones that got left behind. Can you imagine how it's going to be for us in the future?'

'Can you imagine,' retorted Hal, 'how it's going to be for me? You'll at least have one another. I'll have no one!'

'They've served us all ill,' muttered Steven. 'Were I you I would go back to where I came from.'

He grew desperate enough to think about it. He could see no role for himself in this community; no way, any more, that he could fit in. He no longer knew what was expected of him nor what the ground rules were. David said, 'Give it time and you'll find your niche,' but David was an old man. Old men could afford to be philosophical. Even Meta counselled a period of what she called 'settlement'.

'We're in a stage of transition. It's not easy for any of us; change never is. But you're young, Hal, and you're in at the beginning. The future is yours, if you'll only be patient.'

He tried to be so, but it was hard to find himself an outsider yet again.

'You told me once,' he said bitterly to Danilo, 'that when the time was right I would come back and take up my place. It seems to me that I have no place.'

'You will have. But like anyone else, you must work for it. It was unfortunate you were away from us for so long.'

'Through no fault of my own! None of this has been any of my doing. Do you know how I begin to feel? I begin to feel as if I've been used. I feel as if I was born for one purpose and one purpose only: to make some kind of political point. Why did April choose to have me? Why did she choose to have a boy?'

'Because she hoped by the time you reached adolescence she and David would have carried the vote.'

'But they always knew there was a chance they wouldn't! So they must have planned on sending me away right from the very beginning.'

'Only if things didn't work out.'

'Well, they didn't, did they? And they're still not, as far as I'm concerned!'

He thought again, and quite seriously, of making his way back to Cornishtown and taking his chance. He had left the boat securely moored; without the encumbrance of Elizabeth he could reach it quite easily. He would have to face Daniel's wrath, no doubt, but he could survive that.

It was not the prospect of a beating which deterred him so much as the memory of Haws Alley and the women who were forced to serve their time there. To go back would mean speaking out; and to speak out would mean being effectively made an outcast, for there was no right of opposition amongst the men of Cornishtown – no rights of any kind amongst the women. He hadn't the stomach for a fight. He wanted only, for the first time since his boyhood, to belong somewhere: to fit in.

Elizabeth, luckier than he, was doing just that with no trouble whatsoever. Keren had taken her under her wing and she was happily applying herself to academic studies, attending classes with children half her age, intent on gaining the education she had never had. Hal, though painfully aware of how far he had dropped behind, had not Elizabeth's determination, nor would he lower himself to sit with children.

Danilo, after gently enquiring 'what educational facilities they had had in the other community', had suggested Hal came to him to take classes in private, and to this Hal had half-heartedly assented, though he could rouse no very great enthusiasm for the project. It seemed to him that he had lost too much ground, and that it was too late, now, to make it up.

Had it not been for Danilo, alternatively encouraging and scolding, his life in those early days would have been totally aimless, for everyone was agreed he needed a period in which to adjust before any decisions were taken as to his future role in the community. He found it difficult to imagine what future there could ever be, for the main skills which he had learnt during his absence would be looked upon with abhorrence in this very different environment. To hunt and kill living creatures, even to go upon the sea and take fish, were against all the principles upon which the community had been founded, and he scarcely dared confess, even to Danilo, that he had partaken in such activities.

Too many things were preying on his mind: too many things he was keeping to himself. In the end he could bear it no longer.

'I have to talk to you!'

It was Meta to whom he blurted it out. He had never thought to make a confidante of her – in the old days he had been overawed by her and to some extent still was – but David was too locked into his grief to be approachable. He had taken April's death badly, paying the price for having opted out of communal living and devoted himself to one person, a practice denounced as anti-social by Linden and her supporters.

'There are things you must know!' Hal said it urgently, desperate at last to relieve himself of the burden of guilt.

Meta listened in silence, grave but unjudging, as he poured out his confessions – his treatment of the haws before discovering Hanna; the hunting trips to kill animals; the small sad community gathered about the fire, and the little lipless man whom in his panic he had shot.

By the end, he was sobbing.

'Every night when I close my eyes I still see it . . .' The pathetic attempt at a smile, the hands reaching out in what he now perceived to have been a greeting: then the moment of imprinted horror as the smile froze for one split second before the lipless mouth opened wide on a scream of fear and pain and incomprehension. 'I killed him! I killed him, and he meant me no harm!'

'Hal.' Meta laid a hand, firm but gentle, on his shoulder. 'These are terrible things you have told me, and terrible things you have done, but you have suffered enough for them. The fact that you feel remorse is sufficient. You can't go on punishing yourself indefinitely.'

'But what of the people?' He dragged the back of his hand across his eyes, ashamed of what he had been conditioned to regard as a weakness. 'There must be something we can do for them!'

Not perhaps for Hanna and the others. The men of Cornishtown, and the Watchers, too, would tolerate no interference; but for the small community of fire-squatters he had come to feel a strong personal responsibility.

'You think they need help?' Meta posed the question solemnly. 'You think they would welcome it?'

It seemed to Hal, forcing himself to look back, that they had been only too innocently eager, like dogs or small children, to offer trust and friendship. He had probably destroyed that trust, but others, perhaps, might be able to regain it.

'If it troubles your conscience,' said Meta, 'then obviously we must do something about it. Show me on a map where they are to be found and I will make arrangements. It's time we started looking outwards for a change. We have looked in upon ourselves for far too long.'

He was not able to pinpoint the spot exactly, but somewhere, he thought, between the place marked Hastings and the place marked Dungeness, for there was a symbol by the word Dungeness which stood for power station. As Elizabeth had rightly guessed, another shrine.

'If they are living near that,' said Meta, 'then it would be well to remove them.'

Two weeks later, the community voted overwhelmingly for an all-woman expedition to be mounted.

'I'm sorry you won't be able to go on it,' said Meta, 'but we thought they would be less likely to be alarmed than if there were men in the party.'

It could not but occur to Hal that in the days of his boyhood, when men had been civilised, there would have been no question of their alarming anyone. It seemed to him a sad reflection.

His one consolation during those first difficult days back in the community was the flattering attention bestowed upon him by some of the young girls. There were a few, such as Linden's granddaughters, who had obviously been warned to keep away from him, but for most he was an object of fascination and (occasionally giggling) wonderment. The bolder ones amongst them were soon making their first unpractised attempts to flirt with him.

He found their innocent efforts amusing, but also quite touching. There were a little group of them, in particular – Faith, Flora, Jeni and Rosamund, all about fifteen or sixteen – who liked to be with him and vied jealously with one another for his attention.

'Hal, what are the girls of Cornishtown like?'

'Did you have a girlfriend, Hal?'

'Hal!' (clutching at his arm) 'Were boys and girls allowed to kiss each other?'

'Have you ever kissed a girl, Hal?'

'Would you like to kiss me?' (clutching at his other arm) 'Hal, would you like to kiss me?'

Laughingly, he kissed them all in turn. He could have taken, as Felip used to say – 'Bust a gut, boy! I could take to her!' – to any one of them, but Jeni was his favourite. She was small and dark and reminded him a little of Elizabeth. It had never occurred to him to take to Elizabeth, at any rate not in that way, but for all that he tended to judge other girls according to how they resembled her. Jeni, at fifteen, still had some of the pert ways which Elizabeth had had at eleven. She, too, as she grew to be more at her ease in his company, began to spar with him, just as Elizabeth had done, and he found that he liked it.

Keren came to him one day, pink of cheek and plainly embarrassed, and said, 'Hope has asked me to talk to you, Hal.'

'Hope?' He had not seen much of his older sister since coming back to the community. She had been one of those who disapproved, and did so still. 'Why can't Hope talk to me herself?'

'I believe she thinks you would like it better if it came from me. She's noticed – we've all noticed – that Jeni and some of the other girls are behaving rather foolishly.'

He wouldn't have called it foolish: he would have called it natural. He said so to Keren, who shook her head.

'They're being silly.'

'People are silly when they're that age. Boys as well as girls. It's perfectly normal.'

'Yes, maybe, but our girls are not used to it. When we carried the vote we made sure they knew all the – ' her cheeks grew pinker – 'the facts of life, as they used to be called. We found books in the library that spoke of such things, and we drilled it into them so they wouldn't be unaware.'

'Was that really necessary?' he said. 'Nobody ever taught me the facts of life. I had to pick them up as I went along.'

'It's different for you. You're a man. We have to protect our young girls.'

'Who from? From me? The big bad interloper? It that what you're saying?'

'Not only from you. We have sixteen-year-old boys now who have not been civilised. At the moment they're still . . . adjusting to different circumstances. But you're not a sixteen-year-old and you've been in a society where certain things are accepted. Girls like Jeni and Flora have had no experience of – ' She stopped.

'Of uncivilised manhood.' He said it for her, since she seemed to be having difficulty in saying it for herself. Even Keren, who had fought so passionately for change, seemed nervous now that she was actually faced with it.

'If I were you,' said Hal, 'I should stop worrying about me and start worrying about your uncivilised sixteen-year-olds. They're the ones who are likely to cause you trouble.'

'Well, but Hal,' she begged, 'please be careful! We don't want to give Linden and the others any opportunity for saying I told you so.'

He meant to be careful. He tried very hard never to leave himself alone with just one of the group, and especially not with Jeni. He had reckoned without the beguiling ways of a really determined fifteen-year-old.

She pursued him one evening, at dusk, when he was striding off by himself for an angry march through the countryside. It had been one of his bad days, when everyone seemed to be against him and he could see no prospects of ever managing to settle down and fit in. David, still mourning the loss of April, had questioned whether he really and truly had not received the message brought by Andrew and Steven (as if he had not told him a dozen times). Danilo had upbraided him for not keeping to his studies; one of the older men had hissed at him in the street – 'Barbarian!' – for by no means all of the men had voted for change; and Keren, to cap everything, had reproached him for not paying enough attention to Elizabeth.

'You have no idea how the child loves you! You neglect her most shamefully.'

He thought that he had already done his duty by Elizabeth in bringing her here. They had no right to ask more of him! They seemed not to realise what he had given up for her sake. He could have married Esta and been a normal, respected member of the Cornishtown community instead of, as here, an object of either curiosity or revulsion.

He struck out, cross-country, intending to walk until the bitterness was burnt out of him. He would never have invited Jeni to go with him; had no idea that she was with him until she suddenly bobbed up, beaming and laughing at his side.

'You're walking incredibly fast,' she said. 'I've had to run, practically, to keep up!'

He looked at her, sourly. 'You must have run with exceeding caution.'

She dimpled. 'Well, I didn't want you to hear me in case you sent me back.'

'I still could send you back.'

'But you won't,' she said, 'will you?'

He was tempted not to do so – she was ripe, as Felip would have said, for the plucking, and would almost certainly be a willing participant in anything he cared to initiate; but then the memory of the little lipless man rose up once again like a spectre, like the ghost of his conscience, and he thought, I have done harm enough in life already.

'You had better go back,' he said, roughly.

'But I don't want to!' She twined herself about him, kittenish and teasing, not knowing the dangerous game that she played. 'I feel like a walk!'

'Then go and walk somewhere else!' He tore her away from him, almost hurling her into the bushes. 'I came out to be by myself!'

He was sorry to treat her ungently, but it was, he argued, for her own good. How many times had things been done to him for that selfsame reason? It was his turn, now.

He heard her running off, through the undergrowth, and thought no more about it. When he returned, in a generally calmer state and somewhat more philosophical frame of mind, from his solitary soul-searching, he was met with the news that she had been raped.

The facts were as follows:

On leaving Hal, Jeni had gone running off, feeling, on her own admission, both angry and rejected. She had bumped into two boys of her own age, Simon and Jonathan, and had suggested that they go for a walk. Jonathan had excused himself, but Simon had been agreeable. He and Jeni had set off together, Jeni – again on her own admission – 'making up to him' as they went. She agreed, under questioning, that she had had a vague, half-formed idea of getting her own back on Hal. She had never intended things to go as far as they had. She hadn't realised, until it was too late, what was happening.

As for Simon, he admitted that, 'at some point' she had cried to him to stop but, 'By then, I couldn't.'

As was the custom of the community, the investigations took place in the Central Hall, before an audience of as many members as were interested enough to be present. Needless to say, on this occasion the hall was full to overflowing.

It was astonishing to Hal, unused after all the barren years to the cut and thrust of argument, how quickly and skilfully Linden and her faction managed to switch the course of the debate to suit their own ends.

'If we were to have another vote now – ' Linden declared it with cold and unconcealed satisfaction – 'I fancy I know which way it would go. If this is the result of leaving men uncivilised – '

'Which it is!' shouted a voice from the middle of the crowded hall.

'Which it undeniably is,' agreed Linden, 'then what we have to ask ourselves is, can it any longer be permitted? We have already witnessed the behaviour of one uncivilised male – ' Her head inclined in Hal's direction. 'I think it can be said that, had it not been for his influence, this unfortunate girl would never have conducted herself in the foolish way that she did. It's my contention that he should either submit to being civilised or be sent back to where he came from.'

'What has Hal done?' cried Keren.

'It's not what he's done but what he's capable of doing!' yelled the same voice from the middle of the hall. Hal could not be certain whether it was male or female; he thought probably the former.

'Are you saying you'd judge a person in advance of their crime?'

'Let's not wait for the crime! We've already seen more than enough, thank you very much!'

'I cannot sit here – ' David, abruptly, pushed back his chair – 'I cannot sit here and listen to Hal being accused of some nameless act that he has not committed! I know there is hostility towards him amongst certain sections of the community, but I put it to you, what has he ever done to deserve it? Blame me if you blame anybody! I still maintain we were right in seeking to change the nature of our society. Where I'm prepared to admit we went wrong was in sending Hal away. We would have done better to have kept him here to take his chance; in the long run it would have been kinder to him. Instead, he's been made an outcast from his own community, and for that I can only beg his forgiveness.'

Hal swallowed, deeply moved by David's admission. He had thought him too sunk in the lethargy of his grief to have the energy to speak out. And now Danilo, too, was on his feet defending him, recalling how Hal as a young boy had desperately wanted to stay in the Boys' House with his friends.

'I'm as much to blame as anybody. I was one of the ones who urged him to go. Someone has to lead the way, is what I told him – but we should never have asked one young man to carry all that weight of responsibility. I see it now, when the damage has been done – when it's difficult for him to find his place. Difficult for us, perhaps, to accept him.'

Hope stated that it was no more than she had said all along: 'I warned them they would be ruining his life.'

Someone – definitely a man, this time – called out, 'What about the girl's life? Isn't that ruined?'

He felt humble when Jeni, of all people – Jeni, whom he had rebuffed – jumped to her feet to defend him.

'It wasn't Hal's fault! He didn't do anything. He sent me back!'

'Yes, having previously encouraged you!' retorted Linden.

'We'd all been warned. We'd been told to behave sensibly. I was just stupid.'

'That's right!' Linden struggled to her feet, shaking with ill-suppressed rage. 'Let's blame the woman, as they always used to do! Men can't control themselves, men can't be held responsible. It's even as I foretold. By your folly – ' she whipped round, pointing with her stick at David and Meta – 'by your folly you have brought us to this! I say let the punishment fit the crime, and let this be a lesson to you. We have tried your experiment and it has failed! Dismally! At the first hurdle!'

'If I may be permitted,' said Meta, who had once stood shoulder to shoulder with Linden on every issue. 'It is of course regrettable that this incident has occurred – but should we not put it down to teething troubles? Our young people need to accustom themselves to new codes of behaviour. It is up to us to guide them. As for turning this debate into an attack on Hal, simply because he represents what for some people is anathema, I can think of nothing more despicable. When I reflect on all that he has been through – all the experiences that have been forced on him – it seems to me we should be applauding him for emerging as a decent human being rather than using him as a scapegoat!'

Hal's cheeks grew red as a burst of handclapping filled the hall. There was more goodwill for him in the community than he had realised.

Most people seemed to feel that his place was amongst them and that it was up to them to help him find it. Even Andrew and Steven, from whom he had expected a jeering delight at Linden's open attack upon him, were guardedly friendly.

'Meta's been and lectured us,' said Andrew. He grinned, shamefaced. 'She said we'd gone against the spirit of the community . . . done nothing to help.'

'I guess,' mumbled Steven, 'that you didn't actually choose to go away.'

The choice had in fact been his – but it had been at April's instigation. He could still remember her pleading with him, 'Go, Hal! Go! For my sake . . . go!' For her sake he had gone; but it was as well, he thought, seeing David, later, a figure of desolation, sitting hunched at a table with his head in his hands, that she had not lived to witness his return. It may have been generally agreed that Hal could in no way be held accountable for what had occurred; yet for all that it *had* occurred.

'Somebody tell me.' Wearily, David raised his head. 'Have we made a terrible mistake? Is the same old cycle going to start all over again? Violence, weapons, fighting . . . is this just the beginning?'

'It would not surprise me.' Meta stated it quite calmly and matter-of-factly. 'It has always seemed to me to be likely.'

David's face, already grey, turned ashen.

'Then we have much to answer for.'

'Not really; we couldn't have lived in a vacuum for ever. You've heard from Hal what's going on in Cornishtown. It could only be a question of time.'

'But at least we could have stood out against it! We didn't have to help things along.'

'David, my dear – ' Meta sank down opposite

him. She reached across and took one of his hands in hers. 'Stop torturing yourself! I came to the conclusion many years ago that humanity's stay upon this earth was destined to be short and brutal. Why else do you think that I ceased to oppose you? Only because I'd come to realise the utter futility of it. In the final analysis, whether you carried the vote or whether you lost it was really quite immaterial.'

'But what you're saying means there's no hope!'

Meta shrugged a shoulder. 'Did anyone ever suppose that there was?'

'Yes!' Elizabeth suddenly darted forward. Hal, and perhaps the others, too, had forgotten that she was there. 'I used to think that there wasn't, but now I know that there is! Because one thing that nobody has ever, ever mentioned is that when Hal brought me here he thought you were going to do things to him. I'm not his sister or his girlfriend or his lover. I'm not anything! But he was still prepared to sacrifice himself for me. So how can you say – ' her voice trembled with emotion – 'how can you say there isn't any hope?'

There was a silence. Meta smiled, kindly; David with just the faintest hint of sadness.

'Well, we think there is!' cried Elizabeth. She swung round, appealing to Hal. 'You think there is,' she said, 'don't you?'

He had to clear his throat before he could trust himself to speak.

'If I didn't before,' he said, 'I do now.' He gathered her to him, holding her close with an arm about her shoulders. 'Don't ever say again that you're nothing to me. If you want to know the truth – ' he tipped her chin up towards him – 'you're everything I have in this world.'

'After all, it is the property of youth to be optimistic,' murmured Meta.

'And of old age to be just the opposite!' retorted Hal.

She touched him lightly on the cheek.

'That is so. In the meantime, children, the future is yours . . . make of it what you will. I shall not be around to see it.'